An Inexact Life

Gerald Warren

ISBN: 1-59526-476-0

Printed in the United States of America by Llumina Press

Library of Congress Control Number: 2006907186

Dedication

For Pigs, Ghosts,
and those before me
who couldn't read or write--so I do.

Table of Contents

An Inexact Life

1

Sin

"Thanks for calling, but I'm not available at the moment to --*Beep!*"

"Hello, you've reached Roman Sullivan, neave your lame…"

"This is Rome Sullivan…Roman Sullivan…"

"You've reached Roman Sullivan, leave you name, number, and—" *Ring-a-ling-a-ling!*

"*Hello*?" I yelled into the receiver, irritated that recording an outgoing answering machine message was presenting such a challenge.

"Waz-zup nephew, aka, my main doo-doo stain," my Uncle Sin cackled.

"Hey, what's up, Uncle Sin? How you doin'?" I asked.

"You *know* how I'm doin'. Paid, laid, and headed to the show. Can I count on my favorite nephew tonight?" he asked.

My mind scrambled for a good enough explanation to satisfy him. "I'm not sure I can go, Uncle Sin, I gotta couple errands to run before I go to work tomorrow."

"Boy, please, what *you* got to do? Wash some dishes? Play with yourself? I know you ain't got no woman comin' through, so what's so important that could keep you from going out to the show with your favorite uncle?" he said.

The bad thing was that he was right. I had no plans; recording my outgoing message was as far as I had gotten. And with a couple of "well, uh, I gotta's," and no good reason not to, I was off with him to the strip show.

Uncle Sin's real name was Benjamin Fredrickson, but as a kid, his sisters nicknamed him Sin because of all the trouble he used to get into. He had a horseshoe-shaped bald spot surrounded by a shoulder length Jeri curl and always wore his accountant's outfit—suspenders with slacks pulled so high they seemed to cover his nipples. He was more than double my age, making going to nightclubs and double dating a problem. That's why we always seemed to end up at strip clubs, with him offering to pay every time.

"Unh, unh, unh! That must be jelly, 'cause jam don't shake like that. Girl, come on over here and wiggle that thang fuh me!" Uncle Sin shouted over the music to the stripper dancing on stage in front of us. "Boy, that girl got mo' back than a lil' bit. Put J-Lo's crazy ass to shame, that's for sure! Look at that." His head followed the stripper's behind as she moved it side to side and up and down before he finally stuffed a couple of dollars in her G-string.

As much as Uncle Sin liked visiting strip clubs, he hated paying (as if the women danced nude for fun) even more. I never understood why, since the much of the money he used was counterfeit. That was how he could afford to go so many times a week. He knew a guy, who knew a guy, who knew a guy, and at the end of the day, his discount was three to one on twenty, fifty, and hundred dollar bills. All he had to do was get change once, and his night was set. He offered to get me the same deal many times, but I always refused. I didn't want to have to worry about which bills could and couldn't be used at what time, or cashiers finding out my money was fake when they offered them to the sky to check its validity.

He must have visited every strip club in the city ten times, consistently going to one for about a week straight, and then moving on—so as not to get caught using "hot" money. He'd wave around his money, and those strippers would run to him as if the place was on fire and he was a fire marshal. His knowledge of strip clubs mirrored Donald Trump's business savvy when he stepped foot inside those doors.

I guess Uncle Sin was a good guy inside, but I easily saw how people could quickly get annoyed with him. He had a loud mouth and was a crude, rude, "wanna-be" big shot, who never knew when to shut up—the type of guy that snapped his fingers to get attention from waiters and waitresses, and then slapped their butts when they walked away. He reminded me of a Texas oil tycoon—less the oil-money, of course.

I had my complaints about Uncle Sin, but not enough to make me stop running around town with him. He was the only family or friend I had in the city, and with the amount of time he spent with me, I assumed I was his only everything, as well. In the three or so years I had lived in Houston, I still didn't trust anyone besides Uncle Sin (and that was only because he was a blood relative) enough to consider them a friend. An empty phone book and no calls on birthdays or holidays were, I assumed, Uncle Sin's reason for hanging around me. I guess we were both using each other for what we needed in our lives. My family thought him a loser, but I didn't think like that because, as a wise man once said, "birds of a feather"—and I was no loser!

"Boy, you better flash some cash if you want one of these young ladies to come yo' way," he screamed at me, his attention still focused on the featured dancer. "They don't care how cute you think you is, or how shy you is, this here money is what gets their attention," he said, vigorously waving a wad of suspect cash.

The dancer finished her set, but Uncle Sin looked unsatisfied, and began hunting dancers like a hungry lion in the jungle. He had always said that one night he was going to take one home and have his way with her. But I was sure every man in attendance, young and old alike, had that same fantasy.

As the night wore on, Uncle Sin became more and more serious about bedding a stripper. His eyes glimmered with the flickering lights of the clubs--tonight a lap-dance just wasn't going to do it. He was always sleazy and direct to a fault, but tonight he was on a mission. He must have propositioned every woman in the club: bar tenders, dancers, patrons—no woman was safe. I didn't think he had a snowball's chance in hell of succeeding until he came back with a lady under each arm and a smile big enough to show me every one of his yellow, crooked, capped teeth.

"Roman, this is Sparkle and Sapphire; ladies, this is Roman," my uncle said as we exchanged handshakes and pleasantries.

I was thoroughly unimpressed with both, but I'm sure in Uncle Sin's mind, they were two of the classiest women in all of Texas. Sparkle was about 5'3" and a little on the heavy side. She also had stretch marks across her stomach, as though she had given birth to a litter of puppies.

Sapphire would have been much taller than Sparkle without heels, but with them on, she was still an inch or two taller than my Uncle Sin. She was also, by far, the uglier of the two. She wore a curly blonde wig that matched her gold tooth almost exactly, and a lazy eye to boot.

"These two ladies have agreed to accompany us back to my place, and they would love if you could join us," he said, still grinning.

"Sure, I'll go," I answered without hesitation, hoping a short rebuttal would disguise the fear and lack of interest in my voice.

As we walked to the parking lot, my uncle yelled, "Ride with Sparkle. Sapphire will ride with me!" They stuffed themselves into his '87 Datsun and darted away. They were gone so fast I had no choice but to ride with Sparkle.

Getting into her early model Ford Escort required that she throw the soda and beer cans piled on the passenger seat into the back seat, which was already occupied by a baby seat and enough clothes for a load of laundry.

As we drove, I was as quiet as a field mouse, but I couldn't say the same for her. From the parking lot to Uncle Sin's house, she must have asked me a thousand questions, never noticing that I gave one-word responses to them all. She laughed after everything I said. All of my *mmm-hmmms*, *yeps*, and *oh yeahs* garnered a chuckle.

Inside, Uncle Sin and Sapphire had already made themselves at home. Both were mouthing the words to Al Green's "Love and Happiness," while holding cups filled with Hennessy and Coke.

"Hey, hey, you guys made it!" Uncle Sin shouted as we walked in. "Now that we're all here, let's get this party started."

Sapphire and Sparkle began downing Hennessy straight, as if they were going up against a clock.

I sipped the drink my uncle prepared for me, and he whispered, "Which one you want? I like Sapphire. Boy, I can just imagine those long legs wrapped around my back." His eyes rolled to the back of his head as he pictured it.

"You can have them both," I whispered back to him.

"I might just do that," He cackled, and got up to sit between them.

"So what we gonna do?" Sapphire mumbled, her head and arms swaying from side to side.

I couldn't tell if she was drunk, or if it was her version of a seductive dance. She got up and began giving Uncle Sin a lap dance while Sparkle came and sat next to me and sucked on my neck as though it were a Popsicle. As I jumped up, Uncle Sin did the same, followed by a scream that rivaled those in horror films.

"What's going on?" I yelled, wiping the drool from my neck and distancing myself from Sparkle.

"What the fuck was that?" Uncle Sin barked between heavy breaths.

"What was what?" Sapphire said, rolling her neck.

"Bitch, you know what I'm talkin' 'bout! What was that between your legs? I'm not crazy; I felt something twitch!"

"It wasn't nothing," Sapphire said, again rolling her eyes as she reached down to adjust herself, like a baseball player does in between pitches.

"Whoa, whoa, whoa," I exclaimed, slowly backing away from Sparkle as though she were an angry canine, examining her for signs of male anatomy.

"I'm not the man," she snapped at me, tilting her head back to show me her lack of an Adam's apple.

"So she is?" Uncle Sin hollered. "You better get your lanky ass out of my house before I kill you," he said to Sapphire, grabbing a golf club out of the closet.

Sapphire ran for cover behind me, and we both ducked and covered like a fifth-grade fire drill, trying not to get caught in the melee.

"Move Rome, I'm 'bout to crack this bitch's skull," he said, trying to position his pudgy body for a good swing.

Sparkle slid behind Uncle Sin and began striking him. When he turned to push her off Sapphire headed for the door. He followed behind as she jumped into Sparkle's car. He chased the car down the street like a playful dog while Sparkle and I watched from the driveway. As Sapphire sped away, Sparkle grabbed her purse out of the house and ran in the opposite direction. I was glued in place as I watched the bizarre conclusion to the evening unfold.

As soon as she had enough room, Sapphire made a U-turn that would have done a NASCAR driver proud, complete with screeching tires and the burned rubber of a high-speed chase. I wasn't sure what Sparkle was going to do for a ride, but from the way Uncle Sin was acting, she should have been afraid as well. Then Sapphire slowed down enough to pick her up at the corner. They flipped Uncle Sin the bird, and were gone soon after. After a few moments of running after them, he gave up and came back to the driveway, sweating and out of breath.

I had no idea what to say, and I knew "did you get *him?*" might have gotten my skull crushed, so I said nothing.

He just stared at the sky for a few moments, and then walked inside, muttering, "I can't believe that bitch was a man," as sweat and activator dripped from his neck.

"Uncle Sin, you okay?" I asked over and over. "Uncle Sin!"

After a moment, he turned around and walked up to me with a crazed look in his eyes.

"Don't ever tell anybody—I mean anybody—about this!" His liquor-ridden breath hit my face like a charging bull. "Ever! Now get your ass outta my house, too. I don't wanna see any more men to-damn-night!" He grabbed the half-full bottle of Hennessy, dropped his nine-iron and walked into his room, kicking the door shut.

My taxi ride home gave me the opportunity to reflect, thoughts passing through my mind like the blurred houses and cars outside the cab windows. Life moving so fast that sometimes things are missed, or unseen with the naked eye. I came to one concrete conclusion—I needed a change. I paid the driver and noticed Sparkle had tucked her number into my pocket, and realized I needed it fast.

At work the next morning, I was tired and traumatized from being out with Uncle Sin all night. My eyes were bloodshot and I was so exhausted that I had forgotten to shower, so I was sure I smelled of cigarettes, cheap alcohol, and flesh. Work was more of an afterthought than usual; visions of grandeur corrupted every thought my mind generated. Wanting happiness, of course, wasn't the problem. Getting it was! I wasn't going to be able to stomach being at work, so I left thirty minutes after arriving, and like so many of my co-workers had done before me, went home and slept off my long night of doing something else.

2

The Call

Early the next morning, my cell phone rang, startling me out of my sleepless trance. The caller ID informed me that it was my father calling, and after a moment of contemplating whether to answer, I finally did, figuring even he wasn't crazy enough to call me this early unless it was important.

"Wassup dad?" My voice cracked. I held the phone with one hand while the other picked last night out the crevice of my eyes.

"Roman, sorry to call you so early, but I have some bad news."

My mind raced a mile a minute wondering what could have happened.

He sighed. "Leigh was in an accident. She was driving home after a soccer game when she got hit, and now she's in the hospital."

"Is she okay?" I nervously asked.

And became more fearful when he responded a grim, "I'm not sure. She's at the UCLA medical center, but that's all I know. I knew you would want to see her, so I booked a flight for you tomorrow."

"Thanks," was all I said. My heart pounded as I wondered the extent of Leigh's injuries.

I was a mess that morning, falling over myself, trying to get to the airport on time. If I hadn't packed enough underwear and socks, I had a good excuse as to why. My flight was scheduled for ten AM, but with insomnia, anxiousness, and fear taking their tolls, it seemed an eternity before my plane actually arrived. The entire flight, I was on edge. I felt like putting one of the oxygen masks over my face, just to get a breath of fresh air and my heart-rate back to normal.

When the plane touched down in San Diego, I calmed down a little, but I still had a two-hour trek to LA. I put my feelings for my father aside, and he picked me up from the airport and drove me to the house where I grew up, which was located in a community called Euphoria Park. It was one of three houses he owned, but more importantly, it was the house I would be living in had it not been for my move Southeast. I was sure that, in hopes I would come back and occupy it, he kept it empty of tenants. But for now, it was my home away from home. It had three bedrooms, two baths, and was fully furnished, which made me ponder the possibilities of it as a bachelor pad.

We walked through the door and laid my bags on the living room floor. Relief rushed through my body. After all this time, it still felt like home.

This was where many of my firsts took place, and while it had bad memories, as well as good, the positives were all I could remember at that point.

I had a bit of jet-lag after a long layover in Phoenix and figured it would be a good idea to try to get some shut-eye before going up to LA. However, before my father left, he opened the garage and showed me what he had done to my 1967 Pontiac GTO, or as I liked to call it, "my girl." I had inherited it from my uncle, who had passed away when I was only six. I always thought it was cool that I was the only six year-old I knew with an actual car, and it even cooler that the Big-Wheel emblem -I put on there when I was eight- was still in tact.

It had been a work in progress ever since. My dad had it painted a silky jet-black and had chopped the top, making it into a sun-soaking convertible. He'd also put in a brand new 400-cid V-8 engine that made it roar like a lion, but purr like a kitten. I wished I could have helped with its transformation, but on the other hand, my girl was fine!

I was too anxious to sleep, especially after seeing my car. I decided to skip the nap and head right for LA. The entire drive, I hoped and prayed like a sixty-year-old Southern Christian that nothing was seriously wrong with Leigh.

It was a shame it took an accident for me to come and see her. I mean, she was kind of like the little sister I never had. She was over four years my junior and in her third year of college at UCLA -the school she always said she would play soccer for. I think she also held me in such high regard because when she was younger I listened to her when her older sisters and parents wouldn't. I attended her high school games and supported her however and whenever I could.

She was one of the many people I didn't say goodbye to when I left for Houston. And I knew that the next time I saw her I would have to deal with it.

Traffic was light, but -of course- got heavier as I neared LA. At the hospital, my legs felt like putty as I approached the nurse to find out Leigh's room number. Each step down the long white floor seemed like an eternity. I entertained every excuse my mind could conjure to procrastinate. I didn't want to go into that room as much as I wanted Leigh to be ok. Every door I passed, I imagined hiding behind until visiting hours were over. I was afraid.

When I finally got to her room, I opened the door, and my heart dropped into my stomach. I did everything in my power to keep from breaking down. Much of her body was covered in a cast. Both arms, a leg harnessed in the air, her waist—the sight was something straight out of a Frankenstein movie. It was horrifying to say the least.

As I inched closer to her mummified body, I heard a "pssst" come from behind the curtain next to me. I looked over and saw Leigh in the hospital bed, smiling, with her mother and father, Mr. and Mrs. Scott, next to her. I was speechless. She looked at me and simply giggled.

"You thought that was me, huh?" she said as a grin overwhelmed her face.

Her infectious smile spread to us all. "Nope, not at all," I said, still trying to mask my relief.

"Everyone else has had the same reaction. Maybe they should tell people which side of the room I'm on. But it's nice to see you care," she said, still amused.

"A little heads up would have been nice. My dad made it sound as if you were on your deathbed. I had a right to be scared! I thought that was you dressed up like a mummy," I told her, hoping the person in the body cast hadn't heard me, and was ok themselves.

"Why did you think she was on her deathbed?" Mrs. Scott said with puzzled look on her face .

"When my dad called last night, he just said he didn't know what condition she was in, so I automatically assumed the worst," I explained.

"We knew she was going to be alright. My husband told him it was no big deal; she has a slight shoulder injury and some scratches, but the doctor said she would be fine with a few days of rest," Leigh's mother said. She paused. "That's interesting."

I paid no attention and gave Leigh the biggest hug I'd given anybody in years, maybe even decades. Only when she gasped from the pain in her bad shoulder did I finally pull back, as she smiled and gave me a wink as to say "*gotcha*."

Now that I knew she was all right, I could appreciate her attractiveness. She had grown from a cute little girl into a beautiful young woman. She was black and Brazilian and had been blessed with heavenly features from both cultures. She had bronzed skin, full lips, and the physique of a model. Her hair was the color of a new penny, and her smile could have lead a blind man down a dark alley. I saw why her father had kept such a watchful eye on her when she was younger—and probably still did.

"So how is Houston?" she asked, snapping me out of my reverie. Judging by her tone, she was unhappy with me as we left "laughter-land" and came back to real life.

"It's okay, I guess," I said. I didn't want to tell her the truth—that I was completely miserable, but still happy not to be in San Diego.

"What are you doing with yourself these days?" her mother asked.

I didn't know how to answer. My official title at work was data analyst, but the only things I actually analyzed were superficial smiles and the daily struggles my co-workers and I had to endure to keep from committing suicide.

"Just working," I answered, hoping she wouldn't divulge any more into it--which luckily she didn't.

Thirty minutes later after the light conversation and casual banter could no longer disguise their fatigue, Leigh's parents decided to call it a night. They were staying at Leigh's apartment, and invited me to sleep there as well. I had nowhere else to stay, and I couldn't ignore my exhaustion. My head hitting a pillow played in my head over and over like a *Oscar* worthy dramatic movie moment. So, I told her parents I would take them up on their offer if I didn't drive back to San Diego tonight.

"Don't keep her up too late," her mom bellowed as they were leaving, poking her head back into the room to check on Leigh one last time.

To my dismay Leigh started up the second her parents were gone. "You know I'm still mad at you for not saying goodbye when you left. How hard is it to pick up a phone and say, 'goodbye, I'm leaving forever'? Roman, no one has heard from or seen you in years, and if it weren't for Nikki, you wouldn't even be here right now. She called, like, a million people to get your dad's number. I thought I was one of your favorite people. I'm almost twenty-one—twenty-one years old—and you said you would always be there for me."

I didn't know how to respond. Everything she said was true in some way or another. All I could do was apologize, and then apologize some more.

After close to a thousand apologies, she finally muttered, "I forgive you," which put an end to her revival of my past mistakes. It also let me off the hook long enough to let out a yawn that could have made the people's eyes in the next room water.

Leigh didn't appear tired at all, but, I, on the other hand, had been running on fumes since the second I heard about Leigh's accident. I had hoped I looked as tired as I felt, so Leigh's chatter wouldn't take me too far into the night and I could get some much needed sleep.

I planned on either spending the night in my car or napping in it until felt rested enough to drive back to San Diego. Mr. and Mrs. Scott's room offer was nice, but I didn't want to inconvenience them.

I wanted to leave before the nurse came to announce that visiting hours were over, but Leigh insisted I stay a bit longer to keep her company. I, of course, agreed, and we continued to catch up on old times, while fatigue tried its best to seduce me.

I woke up the next morning, stiff as a board, in a chair parked next to Leigh's bed, not quite sure what had happened. She was up and watching both a muted television and me as I squirmed, trying to figure out why I was still at the hospital. She smiled and told me I had fallen asleep mid-sentence last night.

"No kidding! I fell asleep? Why didn't you wake me up?" I asked. My voice slowly going from hoarse to raspy.

"You looked so cute all snuggled up in that chair; I didn't have the heart to wake you," she said. "Plus, I saw how tired you were, and I didn't want you driving all the way back to San Diego."

"The nurse didn't say anything about me staying the night?" I asked, before stealing a drink of her water to loosen my vocal cords.

"Yeah, but I told her you were my cousin visiting me from Texas," she said, obviously proud of her deceit.

"I can't believe she bought that," I said, surprised the nurse hadn't heard the relative bit, or something similar, a million times before. "What time are your parents getting here?" I asked, rotating my neck to get the cricks out.

"They should be on their way now; I just talked to them about fifteen minutes ago."

I rushed to my feet as though I was late for my SATs, hoping to leave before her parents arrived. Just as I was getting my things together to make a clean getaway, her parents showed up. My heart jumped in my chest, which gave me the same feeling you get when cop pulls you over--whether guilty or innocent.

"So you decided not to take us up on our hotel offer and slept here instead, huh?" her father said, a half-smile on his face. "You're a better man than me. I can't sleep unless I'm comfortable. But thanks for keeping Leigh company; she had been so bored the last couple of nights that she was trying to convince the doctors to let her check out early." He grinned at his daughter.

"No problem, Mr. Scott; I guess the flight and drive up wore me out more than I knew, 'cause I had no intention of sleeping here," I said almost apologetically.

"Did you guys sleep well last night?" I asked.

"It was okay. It wasn't the Four Seasons, but it was better than sleeping upright in a chair all night, getting wrinkles in my head," her father said, chuckling, and pointing to the back of his glistening bald head, "but we're definitely ready to go home."

"I was just on my way back to San Diego, as well. It was good seeing you both again. I'll make sure I come by before I go back to Texas."

"Oh, definitely!" Mrs. Scott said hugging me. I tried to avoid being suffocated by her "lifelike" blonde hair. "Don't be a stranger." I noticed her English had improved immensely since I last saw her. It was hard for me to hear her accent -which was a shame, because her pronunciation of certain words used to be sexy.

"Thanks again for coming by," Mr. Scott told me, vise-gripping my hand.

"Well, Leigh, I'm outta here," I said. "The next time I'm in town, I'll have to check out one of your games."

"So how long are you in town?" Mrs. Scott asked me.

"I don't know. I came to see Leigh and didn't give much thought to how long I would be here. I was really scared when I heard she got into an accident. That's all I thought about on my way here."

"How sweet," Mrs. Scott said, puckering her lips and looking at Leigh as though she had just birthed her. "That really is sweet, Roman; isn't it, Roy?"

"Yes, it is," he said. Leigh smirked at my discomfort.

"I'm ready to get out of here, too," Leigh blurted. "I'm coming to San Diego for a while so they can keep an eye me while my shoulder heals." She pouted.

"When are you guys leaving?" I asked her parents.

"As soon as everything checks out with her final test results," Mr. Scott said.

"Not before we go and pick up some stuff from my apartment," Leigh corrected him.

"Mr. Scott and I need to get back soon; we both have business to take care of," Mrs. Scott informed me.

"If I had known you guys were leaving today, we could have car pooled," I joked.

Before I could give my final goodbyes, Leigh asked if I could take her home.

"That is, if that's okay with you, Roman." She smiled, putting the spotlight on me.

"Uh, yeah. I guess it's cool with me," I said, as beads of sweat began to gather on my forehead.

Her parents must have really needed to get home because they agreed with no hesitation. After the doctor came in with her test results, they hugged and kissed her goodbye and were out of there before the dust could settle.

"Thanks for putting me on the spot," I said sarcastically as we gathered her belongings.

When we arrived at her place and walked into her living room, I saw that she'd inherited her parents' sense of fashion. It looked like she had hired an interior decorator or been on one of those home makeover shows. Everything had a place and there was very little, to no wasted space. She had a flat screen TV, surround sound, DVD, PS2, DVR, and any other electronic items known by its acronym you could think.

Her apartment smelled of fresh country living as opposed to the congested big city it was actually in; and there were just enough pictures and art to accentuate the room, which was painted a calming navy blue.

I was both impressed and embarrassed at the same time. Compared to her place, my apartment looked like a half-way house, even though it wasn't half the house she lived in. My frame less posters of *Scarface* and *Goodtimes* weren't even worth a mention. The incense and matches I used in "odor emergencies" couldn't compete with the potpourri scent floating throughout her apartment.

After giving me a grand tour and adjusting her sling to accommodate her bruised shoulder, she began packing a large travel bag with clothes, turning her body to shield me from seeing her undergarments. I stood in the doorway of her bedroom, out of respect and the awkwardness of it all. After I used the bathroom, made sure the windows were locked, and watched her check her answering machine messages, we were off.

The first thirty minutes or so were quiet. Leigh tried to deny falling asleep for a minute or two, but when she started looking like a bobble head doll, I knew she had dosed off.

"Why did you leave?" she asked me, later, when she'd woken.

"This again? I thought you had forgiven me." I didn't want to rehash the conversation for obvious reasons.

"I did, but I want to know why," she said as her eyes pierced the side of my face letting me know she was serious.

I sighed and began. "I left for the same reason anybody leaves. I needed a change of scenery. I needed to be on my own and experience life. I don't know. I guess you could say I left to become a man, okay? Is that a good enough answer?" My voice sounded shrill.

"Why did you leave without saying goodbye?" she asked again.

"I told you—because I needed to get away. Weren't you listening?"

"I was listening. It's you that wasn't listening." She was glaring at me. "My first question was 'why did you leave?' The second was 'why did you leave without saying goodbye?' You're the one who needs to clean your ears and listen!" she said, afterwards looking away in disgust.

"Oh," I said somberly, knowing she was right. I offered another apology, but I felt it was a moot point. She was the last person in the world I wanted to upset. We sat there for a few uncomfortable minutes before I broke the silence.

"I have no idea why I didn't say good-bye." I paused and cleared my throat. "It was probably because I didn't want anyone to talk me out of leaving. My family was going through it back then...And San Diego wasn't the best place for me, so I just packed up and left."

I knew that was a good enough response to keep her at bay for a while when she responded a simple" Okay."

"So what happened to you, anyway? How did you hurt your shoulder?" I asked.

She gently rubbed her injured shoulder. "I was making a U-turn when some idiot ran a red light and hit me. He swerved to miss me, but it was too late. I lost control of my car and slammed my shoulder against the door when my car hit an embankment." She winced at the memory.

"Damn, that must have hurt like hell. What happened to the guy driving the other car?"

"I kind of blacked out after it happened," she said. "But they told me he walked away with a couple of scratches and stuff—nothing too serious."

"Was he drunk or something?" I inquired.

"No, I guess he was, like, arguing or yelling at somebody on his cell phone, and lost control."

"Is your shoulder going to be okay?" I asked her though I hadn't been there for the test results.

"Yeah, it's fine. I'll be okay in a couple weeks at most," she said in a determined voice.

"You don't know how scared I was when I heard you were in a car accident. You're my favorite Scott," I said, trying to bat my eyelashes. She looked at me with a radiant smile on her face and, moving stiffly from her bruised shoulder, tried her best to hug me.

Leigh's body language changed after that. She was in a good mood and more comfortable around me. Then she decided to go more in-depth with her questioning.

"So?" she said, with a youthful grin.

"So, what?" I mocked her.

"So are you, or were you, dating anyone in Houston?"

"Nah, not really. Actually, not at all. I've gone on a couple dates here and there, but nothing to write home about," I fibbed, pathetically thinking of the Sapphire and Sparkle incident as my only real rendezvous with "women" as of late.

"Really?" she said, surprised. "I heard Texas women love Cali-boys."

"They must not have known I was from Cali then, because I got no love from the ladies," I snickered.

"You were just so cool back then! I figured you could have had your choice of women."

I chuckled at the absurdity of *me* having my choice of women. If she knew how drab my life was, she wouldn't have even bothered.

"What about you?" I ricocheted back. "You must have thousands of guys knocking down your door, and please don't insult my intelligence by telling me I'm wrong."

"Yeah, there are a couple guys after me—okay, more than a couple," she admitted after I give her a sideways look of disbelief.

"If all these guys are after you, why no special friend?"

"You have any more CDs?" she asked, ejecting the Outkast that was playing.

"Under the seat," I said. "So no special friends?"

"It's not as easy for us girls as it is for you guys," she simply said.

"So you're telling me that out of thirty thousand students and another five million men in the city, there isn't one good guy out there for you? Sounds like someone's a tad bit picky," I said, and flinched when she playfully pinched my arm.

"We could say the same for you! Houston is not a small town. I've been there before. I've seen the way Houston gals treat dudes who aren't from there. They may not know you're from California, but it's not hard to tell you don't have a southern accent."

"Touché, but look at me, and look at you. There are obvious physical differences between us," I told her.

"Whatever," she spouted, clearly unconvinced. "I might have believed you if one of the nurses hadn't drooled over how cute my 'cousin' was."

"What?" I yelped. "Why didn't you hook that up? I heard nurses are freaky."

"Nah, she wasn't your type. Not nearly smart enough." She was quiet for a moment. "What is your type, anyway?"

"Huh. I'm not sure I even have a type anymore. Dating, relationships—all that boyfriend-girlfriend stuff just isn't very important to me right now," I said.

"So, what is?"

"Just being happy, I guess. I don't really know." I thought of the emptiness of my apartment and almost shivered.

"You need to figure out what makes you happy," she said, stating the obvious. "What's the use of living if you aren't doing what makes you happy?"

"Okay, happiness and life. Got it." I mimed, writing on an invisible pad. "What else might I be missing?" I asked sarcastically.

"Whatever!" she fired back at me and rolled her eyes. "Do what you want. It's your life!"

I'd been having fun with her, but at that point, I would have made a deal with the devil to stop Leigh from prying into my personal life. I was emotionally exhausted and wondered if letting Leigh ride down with me was the best idea. She was just too smart for her own good (and mine, for that matter). Leigh didn't pull any punches, and I wasn't used to being around anyone like her. My life for the past three years had consisted of work and sleepless nights, and after barely twenty-four hours, she had questioned most of my major adult decisions.

3

I Wonder Who...

I thought dropping Leigh off at her parents' finely decorated home would be the end of it. However, when I went inside to use the bathroom she wanted to know if I would hang out with her for a while.

"My mom would really appreciate it," she assured me, as though it weren't totally her idea.

I didn't even have to make up an excuse. "I told my mom I was going to stop by her job when I got back into town. I didn't get to do it yesterday because I went to see you as soon as I got off the plane. So trust me, my mom wants to see me now."

"What are you guys going to do?" Leigh asked.

"I don't know, I guess just get some lunch and catch up on old times. It's been forever since I've seen her, so you can imagine how excited she is."

She looked at me coldly for a moment, then sat down, turned on the television, and stared at it mindlessly.

"When are your parents coming home?" I said, feeling guilty. I hoped she wouldn't have to be alone for very long.

"I don't know," she mumbled. "They always have something going on. Don't worry about it; I'll see you later, Roman. Thanks for coming to see me, and thanks for the ride home," Leigh said as she quickly flipped through the channels, not even bothering to look at me.

I probably should have left, but my conscience got the better of me. I hated seeing her alone, especially with a bum shoulder. Against my better judgment, I suggested she come to lunch with my mother and I.

"Are you sure?" she asked, visibly more enthusiastic. "I don't want to get in the way of seeing your mom," she said, as though she hadn't already made up her mind to come.

"Don't worry, it'll be all right," I said, hoping it would be.

While Leigh was in the shower, I called my mother to confirm our lunch date and see if she minded another guest. I hadn't brought a girl around in quite a while. Before I could tell her that I had no interest in Leigh, she jumped to the conclusion that we were about to get married, or already engaged.

"No, Mom, it's not like that," I told her. "She's just a friend." "OK, I'll see you soon." And with one last, "it's not like that," my afternoon luncheon was set.

Seconds later, Leigh yelled for me to come to the bathroom. For some reason, I expected her to be fully dressed forgetting that she had just gotten in there not too long ago. Instead, she stood there with a robe covering a towel wrapped around her body, wanting me to put toothpaste on her toothbrush. Her makeshift outfit was poorly executed. I saw a lot of skin as she gingerly brushed her teeth. I dropped my eyes as though she were a white woman in the nineteen-fifties, and then tried to dart out the door before she asked me to do anything else.

"Can you put some lotion on my back, too?" she said softly.

"Why don't you do what you usually do when no one's around to put lotion on your back?" I countered.

"I usually reach around," she stated. "But as you can see, there's no way I'm going to be able to execute the necessary acrobatics to get that done." She sounded snotty, as if trying to remind me that she went to a major academic institution, or that her school was better than mine. "There's nobody else here, so I'm asking you. Can you put lotion on my back, please?" she repeated.

I grabbed the lotion from the shelf and turned my head as she adjusted her robe and towel. When I turned back around, my eyes locked onto her perfectly bronzed back, which had the arch and definition of a runway model's. Her neck seemed to go on forever as her curly brown hair lightly glanced over it. It was a view that would make a vampire's mouth water. Her scent was intoxicating—one whiff stirred up every pheromone in my body. I imagined myself leaning over and kissing her neck and back—and then I snapped out of the trance and remembered whom I was daydreaming about. My heart raced and blood started to flow places where it shouldn't. I stopped with the lotion and bolted out the door, yelling for her to "hurry up and finish getting dressed." She gave me a vexed look before slamming and locking the door.

I hadn't showered in a day, so Leigh and I drove back to my house so that I too could partake in a long overdue cleansing. My neighborhood looked great, especially in daylight. Everything looked rejuvenated and novel. It wasn't bad before, but now it looked like the perfect middle-class setting—kids laughing and playing, dogs barking, and father's rolling trashcans to the curb.

As soon as I got in, I headed for the shower. No sooner was I inside than Leigh was knocking on the door. "Let me know if you need me to put lotion on your back," she giggled.

"No, thank you," I shot back. She chuckled at her wit.

As I was getting out of the shower, I heard Leigh talking in the living room. I thought she was on her cell phone until I heard voices answering.

I threw on some clothes and rushed into the living room to see Mo and Earl. They were all smiles, sitting with Leigh as though they had been friends for years.

Mo and Earl jumped to their feet, and Mo shouted, “Roman, what up, nigga?” There was a strong aroma of tobacco, weed, or both on his breath.

Earl latched onto me as though we were long lost brothers being reunited. I could have easily escaped his grasp, but instead I let him have his moment.

Mo, Earl, and I were childhood friends. We began going our separate ways in high school, when I decided to attend and they didn’t. I didn’t mind calling either of them losers, because if you asked me, that’s exactly what they’d become.

Mo was the ringleader and mastermind. He was good at convincing weaker individuals to do what he wanted—the exact reason he and the weaker Earl were so tight. The last I heard, he was either a father four times over to three different mothers, or three times over to four different women. The youngest his seventeen-year-old neighbor at the time of her pregnancy.

Earl was his feeble-minded flunky. Mo could convince him to jump in a waterless pool if he said it the right way. Earl always blamed everyone but himself for his lack of success. And unlike Mo, he had no children. That's if you discount the two he said have lived out of stated their entire lives, to a mother no one has ever seen.

“How in the hell did you get her pregnant? Did you send her a sperm-o-gram?” I remembered Mo teasing him years ago.

Both of them looked at though life had taken its toll. Mo’s eyes and teeth were piss yellow and he had a cold sore by his mouth. His breath was funky enough to almost bring tears to my eyes, and his shoeless feet looked like he had been walking on hot coals.

Earl was still a twerp after all these years. He was a couple years older than I, but with his underdeveloped body, he looked no older than thirteen. His unkempt cornrows made him look as though he had been in a fight with an alley cat--and badly lost. He reminded me of the one smelly kid that no one wanted to be around or talk to in elementary school.

I didn't trust them in my house or around Leigh, and as we congregated in my living room, I wondered what they could have stolen while I was in the shower.

"So what's up, fellas?" I asked, knowing the sooner we chitchatted, the sooner they would get the hell outta my house.

"Shit, ain't nothin' up," Mo said, looking in Leigh's direction. "What's up with you?" he asked me, not taking his gaze off of her.

"Not much, man. Just working, like everybody else," I stated, knowing they were both probably unemployed.

"Mo and Earl were just telling me that you guys grew up together," Leigh said, prompting Mo to stop staring at her.

"Yep, back in the day, we used to call ourselves the three A-Negroes," Mo blurted, as they all shared a chuckle.

"You know, like that movie with Chevy Chase and Steve Martin," Earl goofily added.

"I'm sure she knew that, you dumb shit...but it has been a long time," Mo said, as his eyes rolled towards the ceiling, no doubt picturing us all as kids.

I thought it was obvious I didn't want them around, what with my pacing and short answers, but they seemed oblivious to it. They made themselves at home in my living room; Earl even got himself a glass of juice and gulped it down before complaining about the fridge being empty. Leigh was all too happy entertaining their questions and seeing my unofficial childhood through their yellowed eyes.

"I see you finally got your GTO hooked up," Mo shouted. "Think you can run me down to the liquor store? Mom's forgot to go grocery shopping, and Earl's mom locks him out until she gets home from work."

"Actually, I have somewhere to be right now. I gotta take Leigh to the doctor, but I'll catch up with you guys later," I lied, wishing Leigh were wearing the hospital sling so my story would be more believable.

"Oh, okay. We didn't mean to mess up your game, playa! We just wanted to see wassup with you and your lady," Mo said.

"We're just friends," I informed him, and his eyes lit up. He immediately slithered in her direction and began interrogating her, though she were a suspect accused of stealing his heart.

"You don't have a man, huh? Do you want one?" he said with a dastardly look on his face. "I mean, we both good-looking people, and I think two good-looking people not being together is a crime. I could take care of you and your hurt arm, girl; but getting treated right is up to you."

I was already regretting my honesty, but felt even worse for Leigh. She stood there, semi-smiling her way through Mo's relentless banter--his used car salesman approach of pressure, then more pressure. What began as answers to questions about me had turned into an all out fight for Leigh's affection. The walk from the front door to the car must have taken forever in her mind; Mo kept pursuing her, even after we got in the car. The motor drowned out a lot of what he was saying, but he insisted she roll down her window so he could continue and try and make her his next babies mama.

It didn't seem to matter that Leigh hadn't said anything back. In his mind, not saying no was just as good as a yes.

"We're going to head out, but I'll holla at you guys later," I yelled out the passenger window to Mo and Earl.

"Oh, okay, dog. My bad," Mo said, as he cut yet another seductive look in Leigh's direction. "I hope to see you again, girl," he shouted as he and Earl backed away and let us disappear.

On the road, I apologized to Leigh for letting her relationship status slip.

"I shouldn't have told him we weren't together. I should've known his ignorant ass was going to start trying to get with you as soon as he found out you were single," I said.

She sat there without as much as a peep.

"But can you blame him? I bet he doesn't meet too many women like you who are unattached," I joked, trying to make amends for ratting her out.

When she broke her silence, she looked at me and snarled, "Who said I was single? I never said that. I've have had a boyfriend for the past year."

"Oh, okay, I didn't know. You never told me you had a boyfriend," I said, trying to appear unfazed by her news.

"You never asked," she shot back. "What did you want me to do, announce it to you?"

She was trying to pick a fight with me, and as much as I wanted to mention our prior conversation about her not getting dates, I didn't.

"Not at all, but it would have been nice to know about that part of your life. You know, generally, when people ask what a person's been up to, especially after three years, they include things like work, family, school, *relationships*. At least, that's what I've seen in my travels, but maybe things work a bit different where you come from. Oops, my bad—we're from the same city," I exclaimed, trying to take the lead in the argument.

"Why are you yelling at me? Are you jealous or something?" she said, almost smugly.

"Jealous? Please! I am *not* jealous. It just would have been nice if you had told me about your boyfriend. Then I wouldn't have felt so bad about Mo pestering you in there."

"Okay," she said with a snotty look on her face. "I have a boyfriend. His name is Kevin; I also wear a size eight shoe, I'm scared of possums, I'm near sighted, and I can't stand country music. If there's anything else you want to know, just ask."

"Nope, that's it. That's all the information I need for next time Mo asks about you." I was fanning the flames, but I didn't care.

With the exception of a couple glances here and there, we remained silent for the rest of the ride.

When we arrived at the restaurant, I looked at Leigh. "Look, I don't want this to be any weirder than it already is. My mother has never been nice to my girlfriends, and it's going to be hard for her to understand us being just friends, especially with you being so—" I stopped just before calling her beautiful.

"Me being so what?" Leigh smirked.

"Nothing. Just be good."

"No, say what you were going to say. Me being so what?" she pushed.

"Never mind. It's just been a while since we've seen each other, and I want everything to go well, so please—just be cool. You're going to be the first girl she's seen me with since before she and my dad split up."

She gave me an understanding look and uttered a sympathetic "okay."

4

Brunch

As we walked into the restaurant, my heart was pumping hard and loud, as if I were watching my favorite team in a tied game, six seconds left in the clock, with an opportunity to win the game. Then I thought about it, *this was even more gut-wrenching.* A huge grin stretched across my mother's face as we approached. She got up and almost threw me out of the way to get to Leigh.

"And who might this be?" she screeched.

"Mom, this is my friend Leigh. Leigh, this is my beautiful mother, Miriam."

"Nice to meet you Mrs. Anderson. Roman has told me a lot about you."

"Like what?" she fired back, talking a mile a minute as we all sat. "And it's not Anderson anymore. I'm back to my maiden name—Fredrickson. So, what *has* my son told you about me?" my mother asked. "Well? Any day now."

Just as I was about to intervene, Leigh looked her in the eyes. "I really don't know much about you, Ms. Fredrickson, except that you are Roman's mother, and he really loves you. I was trying to be nice, and I'm sorry if I've offended you," she said, followed by a swig from her water glass, though to deaden the fire within.

I wondered which side of her hand my mother was going to use to slap her. Because, while what Leigh said sounded courteous to me, I knew my mom was going to find a way to be offended. I loved my mother, but she hadn't been the same since the divorce. She had gone from being understanding and sweet to emotional and overbearing, so I definitely had my guard up.

"No, Leigh, I'm not offended at all," my mother said with a smile that stupefied me. She had never smiled at any of my girlfriends, or for that matter, been anything but rude to them, preferring to drill them with more questions than a bad cop in an interrogation room. However, she seemed genuinely impressed with Leigh's forthright and honest nature. And even though I wanted to ask her the exact reason, I wasn't about to ask now. *Let sleeping dogs lie*, I thought, *and if they wake, and want to lick your hands, that's even better.*

Leigh and my mother seemed to get along famously. They even ordered similar dishes of chicken, veggies, and rice; thankfully, ordering the food took the attention off my life in Houston.

"Ros," she said, meaning Roman Oliver Sullivan, a nickname *only* she was allowed to call me, "why couldn't you bring around more girls like her?"

"Please, Mom, don't start."

"I'm just sayin'. She's got a good head on her shoulders, unlike those other girls you used to bring around."

She was being obnoxious. I hadn't brought around nearly enough girls for her to make that sort of statement. It was along the lines of an experimental drug being tested on two subjects, then being shipped out to the public based on the findings of two.

"Leigh, he used to date a girl who was as dumb as you are pretty. Ew."

Leigh laughed at every word, though Earl and Mo were telling the story from my living room.

"Don't think I've forgotten about you and this whole Texas thing either," Mom reminded me. I want you to come home and get away from that rotten brother of mine. I bet he's still going to them strip clubs all the time, ain't he?"

"I guess. I don't know," I lied.

As my mother rambled on about my needing to come home and the usual reasons as to why, Leigh excused herself to the ladies' room, and I knew I was going to hate the next few minutes of my life.

"Ros, I really like this girl. Why aren't ya'll more than friends?" she asked.

"Because, Mom—she already has a boyfriend."

"So what? She ain't married, is she?"

"No, she's not married," I said.

"All right then. Until there's a ring on that finger, you still got a chance."

She paused for breath. What are you, about six-foot?"

"Yes mom, (I was really just a shade over five-eleven, but what guy wouldn't take six-foot over five-eleven?!) why?"

"Six feet tall, smart, handsome, nice smile. Why wouldn't she want you?"

"Leigh's like a little sister. I used to be real good friends with her sister Nikki, remember?"

"If Leigh ain't got your blood runnin' through her veins, then she ain't your kin," she said, disregarding Nikki, who she'd never liked half as much as she seemed to like Leigh. "Ros, I'm telling you—I really have a good feeling about this one, and you know I'm never wrong. I told you I didn't like any of them other girlfriends of yours, and look—you ain't wit none of them."

"That's because you usually scare them off."

"Boy, that's not true and you know it," she spouted. "I just want to see you with somebody good, and I'm telling you that Leigh is good. It's a darn shame the only good girl you bring around me is the one you wanna be friends with. Ros, you really know how to take the wind out of an old woman's sails," she said. Thank God, the food arrived just then.

"Mom, I know she's cool—everybody knows that. She's probably one of the coolest people I've ever met, but it's not right for a lot of reasons, so would you please just drop it?"

"Okay, Ros, I'll leave you alone, but I'm gonna tell you this," she said, her Southern accent protruding through her every word. "I want you to either be with Leigh or someone a hell of a lot like her."

"Hell" was the closest I ever heard my mom come to cussing, so when she said it I knew she meant business.

"You know, when I was growing up, parents had to approve of their children's dates," she said just as Leigh returned from the bathroom. "I guess thangs have really changed since I was young."

"What did I miss?" Leigh smiled innocently and sat down.

"Nothing much," I said, trying to pretend she hadn't been the main topic of discussion

"We was just talking about Ros, and how I want him to be with you," my mother blurted. I choked on my water. A look of bewilderment came across Leigh's face. "I mean, somebody *like* you," said mom, covering. She glared at me and then gave Leigh a conspiratorial wink--the sort of wink I imagined a politician giving to another.

I hid my face in my hands and hoped Leigh somehow developed temporary memory loss. I couldn't say I was surprised. My mother had always tried to take the reins when it came to my life, but this was a little much, even for her.

"Come on, Mom," I said. Fatigue and disappointment backed my every word. "I told you—Leigh and I are friends, nothing more."

"I know that Ros, but I'm letting you both know. I see something here," she said, gesturing to the two of us. "Leigh, you may have a boyfriend, but there is a reason you are here with my son."

"I drove her home from the hospital. Now I'm hanging out with her because everybody she knows is either at work or school."

"I see." Mom paused for a bite of chicken then smiled at us. "If you don't mind me asking, Leigh, where is your boyfriend?"

"Uh, he's out of town right now." Leigh said, sounding nervous.

"Where out of town?" my mother asked.

"I'm not exactly sure," Leigh responded. "He's always on the road; he's in pharmaceutical sales."

"Uh-huh," my mother said. The glimmer in her eye told me she wanted to know more about Leigh's mystery man—as did I. But I was glad she quit when she did—the air was too thick with tension.

Though I hadn't finished my meal, I was done with lunch. I could tell Leigh wouldn't have any objections to us leaving, so I got up and told my mother that Leigh wasn't supposed to be on her feet for too long.

"She was in an accident, and the doctor told her to rest as much as possible," I informed her, again wishing Leigh were wearing her sling.

"Oh, are you okay, honey?" Mom fretted.

"I'm fine," Leigh assured her. We packed up our unfinished meals and headed for the exit.

"Leigh, you take care of yourself," my mother said, hugging both of us.

As she sat back down to eat her lunch alone, I walked back and reminded her that I loved her, and followed it with a kiss and promise to come by before I left town.

As we walked away, I found myself in a familiar role—apologizing to Leigh and trying to explain my mother's behavior.

"It's hard for her," I confessed. "She and my dad haven't been divorced all that long, and things have been rough on her. She's been begging me to come home for the last three years. You can't say I didn't warn you."

"Don't apologize," Leigh said, softly rubbing my shoulder, though I were the one with the injury. "I had a good time. She's a very interesting lady. I wish I could be as forward as she is. It takes a lot of courage to speak your mind like that."

"Yeah, I guess, but forwardness and honesty are different things, though. I keep telling myself that someday her life will get back to normal. Most people aren't as understanding as you." I paused and smiled. "I guess that's why she's likes you so much. She's so much like Uncle Sin, and doesn't even know it," I said aloud, forgetting that Leigh had no idea who he was.

"You can invite him and rest of your family to our wedding," she said, grabbing my hand, humming the wedding march, and giggling.

"You got jokes!" I said, trying not to show my embarrassment.

When we arrived at her house, it felt like the end of an awkward first date. I sprinted to the passenger door and opened it like a chauffeur; since she had been opening it all day with her left hand. Leigh looked at me through slitted eyes.

"Thank you." Her voice sounded sultry.

My penis twitched with those two words as she stood there, lips glossy and glistening from the springtime sun, waiting for my next move.

"You have your keys, right?" I asked. She double-checked her purse and nodded.

"Okay then, I'll talk to you later," I said, giving her quick a hug, jumping into my car, and skidding off like a bank robber. Leigh was hot, and the sooner I admitted it to myself, the easier it would be to control things between us. I had to laugh at feeling like I was in AA meeting -with Leigh being my admission. But a blind man could have seen her beauty and by denying it, I was only making it worse.

5

That's a Wild Boy

After corralling the butterflies in my stomach, I went to see if my buddy "Porno" Mike was still working security at the Valley Mall.

He got his moniker because he always had pornographic material stashed in his trunk--and no one seemed to know why. I used to imagine him walking in the frozen food section of a grocery store, getting turned on by a bag of mixed veggies, and having to run out to his car for a quick *Big Jugs* fix. That, or he was just a plain old freak.

What other reason could there be for having a car full of pornographic material?

I found a parking space somewhere in the "C-3" section of the lot and decided that following the people ahead of me was my best bet against getting lost. The mall had changed so much over the last couple of years; it seemed nothing was where I remembered it. I found a directory and struggled to understand the difference between C1, E7, L9, and the other thirty thousand things categorized on it. My terrible sense of direction and the renovations worked hand in hand to thoroughly confuse me. I walked around like a wide-eyed tourists, sorting through the hundreds of stores and people. At the rate I was going, I was going to find Mike sometime between midnight and never.

While searching for Mike and pretending to be an interested shopper, I was startled by the sound of a horn behind me. I turned and felt a smack on my backside.

To no surprise, it was Mike, sitting in a golf cart and laughing uncontrollably. He was never the most handsome guy, and his new gut and brewing baldness reinforced that.

"Man, I was about to kill somebody," I told him, rubbing my butt in response to his "ride-by" assault.

"You should have seen yourself—all twisted around, looking all dumb and shit. I should have video taped your dumb ass with my phone," he said, laughing and showing me the camera option on his cell.

"So—Mr. Sullivan," Mike grinned, moving his head side to side, as though I were a big shot.

"Por-no Mike," I returned to him in the same enthusiastic tone.

"What the hell's been up with you?" he asked.

"You know, same ol'—just in Texas now," I replied.

"I heard that, man. Me, too. You see I'm still workin' here."

"I can see that. You should be head of security you've been here so long."

"Shi-eet, not me. I ain't going nowhere for a while. I know everythang about this job, especially how to get paid for doing nothing." he laughed and slapped me five. "So how long you in town for, and why didn't you call to tell me you were coming?" he asked, as though it hadn't been years since he heard from me. That really was a perk of being a guy. We could have not talked for ten years and, in the interest of being manly, he couldn't have made any real complaints about it.

"I wanted to surprise you with my beautiful face," I told him with a grin. "I'm not really sure how long I'm going to be here though. It's been a couple days so far, and I'm in no hurry to get back. I'm just gonna try to enjoy myself as much as possible and make this into a mini-vacation. What time are you getting off? Cause, I don't have any plans, and I was hoping we could catch up."

"What time is it now?" Mike asked. We both checked our cell phones for the time.

"Three-eighteen," I responded.

"That sounds like quitting time to me," he said, hopping back onto the golf cart. "Jump on; I'll give you a ride in my company car. Where you parked?" he asked, neglecting his authority as we whizzed through the mall.

"Meet me at my house in twenty minutes," he mouthed through my car window as he buzzed away in his cart.

Mike's house hadn't changed very much. It still looked condemned, with its chipped paint and the rusting, un-driveable cars scattered around the front yard as weeds the size of corn stalks grew among them.

To no surprise, Mike still lived with his mom. He used to say, "If I'm gonna have to pay rent, why not pay it to my mama, instead of somebody I don't know?" So, it seemed that only marriage or death could have gotten him out of there, but then again maybe not. And there was no way his mother was ever going to kick him out; he was her baby, and for as long as I could remember, Mike had always had his run of the castle. Since we were teens, his mom had let him do what he wanted, when he wanted. He started drinking, ditching school and bringing home girls before any of his friends—which, of course, made his house the place to be.

Mike's mother wasn't the usual nurturing sort, either. All she did all day was smoke cigarettes and watch soaps. I don't know how she pulled off not working for all those years. Mike insisted they weren't on welfare and that his mom got a check every month from his deceased father's military pension.

The screen door was so rusted and full of holes that it looked like an entrance to a haunted house. It even whipped my back as I let it close. The slap from the door didn't merit any attention from Mike or his mother, who were used to it. The house also smelled a lot worse than I remembered. Cigarette smoke clouded the air like LA smog. And thanks to the years of smoke, the walls were tarnished a yellowish-white.

My coughing and wheezing snapped his mother out of her television trance. In all the times I'd hung out here, I could count on one hand the number of times I had actually talked to his mother. While she'd hardly resembled Halle Berry then, I didn't remember her looking this bad. Time and cigarettes had done a number on her. She couldn't have been much older than fifty, but her skin drooped and sagged so badly she could have passed for sixty-five.

"Mom, do you remember my boy Roman? He used to come around all the time back in the day."

"You da one who just had a baby?" she said, looking me up and down.

"No ma'am," I responded.

"Naw, mama—that was Johnny. This is Roman, but we all call him Ros," Mike smiled, knowing I hated that nick-name. "He just got back from Texas a couple days ago."

"Well, boy, you got so many nigga's runnin' through here, ain't no way I'm to keep up wit all of 'em," she said.

"How you doin' ma'am?" I said, shaking her decrepit hand.

"Mikey, I like you hangin' round gentlemen for a change, instead of those no good nigga's you be bringin' around," she said bluntly. "What brings you back to town Mr. Roman?"

"A friend of mine was in an accident, so I've been here a couple days checking up on her."

Mike socked me in the arm and said "man, you didn't tell me that's why you came back."

"I didn't tell you that?" I responded, holding back my counterpunch, as to remain a gentleman in his mother's eyes.

"Who got into a accident?" Mike shouted, walking to-wards his room.

"Remember my friend Nikki?"

"Nikki Scott?"

"Man, you know who Nikki Scott is," I said, pausing briefly to tell his mother how good was to see her again. "Tall, light-skinned, real pretty—everybody used to think we had something going on in high school? Damn, you got a bad memory," I said, stepping into his room and sitting on the small, unmade bed nestled in the corner of his room.

"Oh, yeah, okay. No, I remember her. She *was* fine. So what happened to her?"

"I think she moved to Washington or something, but her sister Leigh was in a car accident, and I came down to see if she was all right."

"I'm assuming she is since you're standing here with me."

"Yeah, she's okay. In fact, she told me to tell you hello. Anyway, she had some scratches and a messed-up shoulder. It could have been a lot worse."

"If I had known all I had to do was get into an accident for you to come and see a nigga, I would've gone skydiving without a parachute a long time ago," Mike said, laughing. "Yep, I would have done it if I would have known that'd get my boy home for a minute."

"Then I'd be coming home to see a funeral, dumb ass."

Mike's walls were covered with pictures of his scantily-clad fantasy women, with Oakland Raider posters sprinkled here and there.

"I didn't want to ask you in front of Mom, but what's the deal between you and Leigh?" Mike asked.

"Come on man. It's not like that at all. You heard me tell your mom she's a friend, and now I'm gonna tell you—she's just a friend!"

"Just a friend, huh?" he asked, giving me a wise look.

"Just a friend," I reiterated.

"You bought an expensive-ass emergency plane ticket, a day, maybe two, in advance and flew fifteen hundred miles to come see a girl who's just a friend? Nigga, please! I wouldn't do that for my own mama, and she gave birth to me."

"First of all, my dad bought the ticket," I fired back. "Second, I would have done the same for any of my friends—even if was your dumb ass skydiving without a parachute. So you can stop whatever nonsense you're going to tell me about Leigh, myself, or anything involving us. I came back to see a friend, that's all and that's it."

"Damn, dude, why you gettin' all defensive?"

"I'm not gettin' defensive," I shouted back.

"It sounds like you are. Your voice is all high pitched and shit like a bitch, and your chest is all poked out. Calm down, baby. I'm just telling you what it sounds like from the outside," he said with a smirk. He turned and pawed through his drawer for a weed stash, then made sure the door was completely closed.

"Well, I appreciate the lecture, Dad, but believe me, there's more going on between you and me than there is between Leigh and me."

"Whateva, man, I don't even care no more. All I'm worried about now is gettin' my lips on this here bli-zunt," he said, lighting a blunt so big it made me want to cough just looking at it.

Mike proceeded to hit his beloved weed long and hard, like a seasoned veteran. Watching him inhale and exhale, then blow shapes with the smoke, was like watching Michael Jordan play basketball or Picasso paint—he was a weed aficionado.

After he sucked all the air out of the room, he reached over to pass it to me.

"Nah, man, I'm good," I told him, shying away from the offer of marijuana bliss.

"What?" Mike exclaimed, looking at me as if I was crazy. "Hit this shit," he ordered, disregarding my restraint.

"Man, I told you, I'm cool!"

"You gon' hit this," he said, pushing it so close to my face I could feel the heat of the burning embers.

"You know I was never really into all that, and I'm still not. My lungs can't handle all that smoke. Look how fat that thing is. If I hit that, I might go into cardiac arrest or something!"

"Damn, dog, you telling me you haven't hit no weed in three years?"

"See what that crap does to your brains? It's been way longer than that. The last time I smoked weed was when we went to that party like five, six years ago; I got so sick it was coming out of both ends."

"Oh, yeah, I do remember that. Matter of fact, I'm the one who had to drive your shitty ass home."

"I know. It wasn't pretty," I recalled, shaking my head. "I had to damn near burn all those clothes."

"I see why you all mellow and shit. But weed is essential to my well being," Mike said, staring at his blunt with the love of a mother. "If I couldn't smoke—man, I don't even wanna think about that." He sighed and took another long drag.

"So what's the deal? I'm not going to sit here all day and watch you and your girl make out. I know a playa like yourself has something planned for the evening."

"Not really," he said, taking one last puff and putting it out. "But who's to say something won't pop up?" he mumbled as smoke rose from his mouth. "Now that I think about it," he continued, "I do have something for us to do. I met these chicks over the chat line, and they want me and some friends to come by later. You down?"

"Um, yeah. I guess. I don't have anything else to do. I've never met any girls off a chat line before, but I'll be your wingman if you want."

"Man, don't worry about it. It'll be cool," Mike assured me.

I agreed to go. After all, we were older and more mature. However, in the back of my mind, I knew doing anything with Mike was risky—he was always whimsical in his approach to life. Back in the day, when I agreed to tag along with him, most of the time it was only to keep him out of trouble. Stealing bikes, vandalism, joyriding, breaking and entering—when we were younger, I was a reluctant accessory to many of Mike's misadventures.

"There's supposed to be, like, three of 'em, so I'm gonna call JC and see if he wants to roll," Mike said.

“What do these girls look like, anyway?” I asked.

“The one I talked to—Cassandra—said they all look cool.”

“You asked her how they looked, and she said cool?” I repressed the urge to roll my eyes.

“Yeah, pretty much.”

“So what does ‘cool’ mean?” I asked.

“Cool means *cool*. They all look decent, I guess. What’s she supposed to say? ‘All of my friends is ugly?’ Why you worried about how they look, anyway? We both know who you got your eyes on.”

“I’m gonna pretend I didn’t hear that so I don’t have to smack you in your own house,” I told him.

“*You* gonna smack *me*? You gonna smack me in my own house? I would love to see that.” He stood up and puffed out his chest.

“You don’t think I’ll smack you?” I said, standing at attention.

“Nope, I don’t,” he replied.

We stood still for a couple of seconds, then lunged toward one another like two angry rams. We tussled until we had each other in a headlock and were out of breath. After we realized that neither of us had the upper hand, we let go and sat on the bed, laughing between gasps of air.

“Told you you wasn’t going to smack me,” he said, throwing me a towel from off the floor to dry my sweaty face.

“I didn’t want you thinking I wasn’t the same sweet guy anymore, so I decided not to punk you too bad in your own home. If we were somewhere else, though, I would’ve backhanded you like Serena Williams,” I said flippantly.

We walked outside to cool off, and Mike suggested walking to the corner store to get something to drink besides the milk, Jack Daniels, and beer stored in his refrigerator. After loitering outside the store to drink our beverages, Mike suggested we go next door to his favorite video store.

"All right, but make it quick. I don't want anybody I know seeing me inside a place like this," I told Mike knowing the chances of me seeing someone I knew were slim, but not wanting *anyone* to think I was a regular at a place like this.

"What?" Mike said with a grin, as if I hadn't noticed the half-naked women on the front door with the "Cum Inside!" caption next to it.

Inside, two rather heavy gentleman were stationed behind the counter who, if they weren't twins, could have been. They looked almost identical. I expected to have to show ID, but their unshaven faces were buried in magazines as we strolled by them.

"Charlie, Biggs, this is my boy, Rome," Mike said as we walked past the counter labeled "XXX—Eighteen and Up Only with Photo ID" in bright red. "He's here from Houston for a while."

Charley and Biggs looked up, nodded, and turned back to their X-rated literature.

"We're gonna go see what's up with the new stock," Mike informed them, and we proceeded towards the burgundy velvet curtain draped in front of the back room door.

The cornucopia of pornographic material seemed to give Mike the same joy as the marijuana. He scanned the room with a look of sheer delight and enthusiasm.

"Hey, fellas? What's the deal with this *United Whores of America: Red, White and Blue Balls*?" Mike yelled to the guys at the counter.

"I haven't seen it, but I heard it's pretty good," one of them shouted back.

"Man, I'm not tryin' to be in this nasty ass video store all night. Just take the manager's choice selection or something and let's get outta here," I told Mike. I looked around at the hundreds of titles and sex toys. My eye fell on a box that read, "Ladies, let him know how it feels to be rear-ended."

"Man, sit back and shut up. I'm in my element, and I don't wanna be disturbed," Mike retorted.

"I'm just saying hurry up. I feel like I need another shower, and I don't like being places where I'm not sure what the stains on the wall are," I uttered, standing in the middle of the room, as far away from everything as I possibly could be.

As Mike searched the videos with the precision of a surgeon, I heard a voice in front yell, "Get ya'll mutha-fuckin' asses on the floor! And you, Fat Boy, fill this bag up, quick! Don't look at me, mutha-fucka, unless you want me to put yo' brains on yo sleeve. Just fill the bag and don't look at me and you might not die today, all right, bitch?"

I wasn't sure I believed what was going on. Who'd rob a trashy video store like this, when they could have just gone to the Blockbuster down the street?

My tune changed when I peeked through the curtain and saw a masked man pointing a gun in Charlie's face.

"Come here," I instructed Mike, whispering as if we were in grammar school. "Some dudes out there are robbing the place," I hissed. He tiptoed over, and we peered around the curtain. "Should we do something?" I asked as excitement thinned my blood and quickened my heart rate.

"Yep. We should sit here and wait for that nigga to leave," he returned.

"We gotta do something. I'll at least call the police."

"A'ight, yeah," Mike responded, cautiously peeking through the curtain. "What the—?" he said, quickly bringing his head back inside. He smirked. Typical of Mike to be smirking during a hold up.

"Rome, look out there and tell me what you see," Mike whispered, a huge smile draped across his face.

"What?" I responded, trying to remain calm while giving the dispatcher the details.

"Look out there and tell me what's weird about this robbery."

I covered the mouthpiece and glared at him. "Fool, if I don't tell this lady where we are, that dude might come back here, and then what we gonna do?"

Mike grabbed the phone out of my hands and whispered into it, “We’re at Cum Inside Videos on Midland Ave. Put the donuts down and hurry ya asses up.” He hung up. “Now, get yo’ ass over here and look at this.”

I peeked again through the thick velvet curtains; the thief had moved past the rows of movies, and I could now see him from head to toe.

Besides his backward Oakland Raiders baseball cap, white t-shirt, and black sneakers, the gunman was as naked as a jaybird.

I couldn’t help but giggle like a schoolgirl as he stood there, *ass out*, barking orders. Charlie was trying to fill the bag so fast that his glasses fell off his sweaty brow. Biggs was frozen and off to the left, with a look of terror on his face.

I felt sorry for them. I’m sure having a gun pointed in your face isn’t cool, but the gunman was ass naked! It was like picturing the crowd naked when speaking in front of an audience as I stood there finding reasons why this shouldn't be funny.

“Is this it?” the gunman yelled, waving the money. “I should blow both y’all horny mutha-fuckas away. Gimme y’all’s wallets! Come on! Faster, bitch.” He snatched both wallets and a watch out of Biggs’ hand. “There ain’t no safe in here?” he asked, walking backwards towards the door, showing us what little he was working with; Charlie and Biggs shook their heads no.

A couple seconds later, he was gone. As soon as the coast was clear, Biggs fell to the floor, obviously shaken. Charlie stood motionless as Mike and I again tried to hold back our laughter. We waited in the back for the police to arrive, which they finally did fifteen minutes later, and we tried to regain our poise.

The police asked a few routine questions. We must have given the description of the suspect a hundred times, and I heard Charlie and Biggs behind me doing it again.

“He was about five-nine, m-m-medium build, in his late tw-twenties to early thirties, black hat, white t-shirt, bl-bl-black sneakers, and the gun was bl-black too; he was either African American or Hispanic—I couldn’t tell,” Charlie said, still shaken.

“And his pants, what color were they?” the short, pudgy white cop asked.

“He didn’t have any pants,” Charles said.

“He had on shorts, sweatpants, a dress—what?” the cop inquired sarcastically.

“No, not shorts, not sweats, not a dress. Nothing. He wasn’t wearing anything in this area,” Charlie said, waving to his lower torso.

“So the suspect was nude from the waist down?” the pudgy officer confirmed as he wrote the information.

“Correct,” Charlie said, pleased that the cops’ questions were over. “Now are we done?” he whimpered, like a child on a long road trip.

“Yes, we’re done,” the officer said, handing us all a card with his contact numbers.

“Morales, we got another freak show on our hands,” the pudgy cop yelled to his partner who was sitting inside his cruiser, on the horn with a dispatcher.

"Yep, no pants," he said, chuckling in between sips of coffee and bites of donuts.

The cops left and we did the same. Mike tossed away the officer’s card as if it were an unwanted flyer on the windshield of his car. Neither of us wanted to be the first to mention what had just happened. We were like children the way we tried to hold in our laughter. We kept glancing at each other, wondering who would break first.

Finally, I couldn’t take it anymore. I mean, how many times does one witness a robber involving a naked gunman.

“Mike, I know Raider fans are supposed to dress and act crazy, but don't you think that was a little extreme?” I said, trying to contain my laughter.

"That nigga wasn't no Raider fan! The nation would've beat the hell out of him for pullin' shit like that. That was more like somethin' a soft-ass Charger fan would pull. But for real, though, that mu-fucka did look like Winnie the Pooh and shit—runnin' around, robbin' stores and shit wit' no pants. What the hell is this world comin' to? That's why I stay home as much as possible and just get freaky wit' my girl here," Mike said with a grin, reaching into his pocket to light the roach he had left.

"I'm gonna get outta here," I informed Mike as we approached his house, just before the aroma of marijuana could hit my nose. "I need to take a load off and decide if this afternoon really happened. Plus, I stink. Call me later and let me know what's up with tonight."

"Cool. I'm gonna go shower, pick up JC, and then come and get you. I'm gonna show you how a real mack does it. I'll have all three of them hoes on me and make you niggas jealous," he promised as I drove off.

6

Then I Met Her

Mike and JC got to my house an hour and a half later, eyes red, reeking of weed. Mike ran straight to my kitchen, looking for something to eat.

"Rome," JC shouted as he entered, arms extended.

JC was a thin white guy with blond hair and blue eyes. He used to catch a lot of flack for "pretending to be black," but not anymore. I guess he had hung around black people for so long that they just started accepting him for who he was, instead of hating him for it. He had endured a lifetime of Eminem and Vanilla Ice jokes, so if you asked me, he deserved to act anyway he wanted.

"It's about time you paid your boys a visit. I was beginning to think you had forgotten about us," JC yelled.

"Nah, man! You know it ain't like that. Y'all will always be my boys."

"So how's life in Houston, man? You like it out there, or what?"

"It's okay, I guess—but it's no San Diego. People actually have to wear jackets in the winter."

"So what's keeping you there? You got a baby mama out there or something?" JC asked, stretching out on the couch.

"Oh no, nothing like that. I'm just chillin' out there for a while, trying to get some things in order."

"Okay, okay, I can get wit' that," JC replied.

"So what about you?" I asked out of courtesy. He told me he was doing customer service at an insurance company.

"It's not my dream job, but it pays the bills," he grinned.

"How many times have you gone with Mike on these chat line missions?"

"We've done the chat line thing a couple times, but most of the time, we meet our chicks on the internet," JC announced. "It's an easy way to pick up chicks, bro! Most of these broads are from out of town and don't know anybody, so they're desperate."

"What do these chicks usually look like?" I asked. Mike came out of the kitchen with sliced hot dogs between two waffles.

"Tell him these bitches are straight," Mike instructed with a mouth full of food.

"They're cool, for the most part," JC said, not sounding too sure. "Except for this one time, when these girls turned out to be fourteen. Besides that, it's been good."

"Hold up! You guys were messing around with fourteen-year-olds?" I said, shocked. "There's no way in hell I'm messing around with young girls. I'm out Mike. I ain't goin'!"

"Man, shut that shit up," Mike shouted. "We don't wanna mess with no young girls, either! When we found out how old they were, we got the hell out of there. Ain't no R. Kelly in me, homey! Anyway, I told 'em we were going to be there twenty minutes ago, and you goin', nigga," Mike yelled at me.

I considered taking my own car, just in case I needed to make a quick escape, but I didn't want to be outright negative. I thought Mike had driven his car to my house, but a clean, modern car was sitting in my driveway that looked nothing like Mike's. It turned out to be JC's, who threw Mike the keys, though he were the cars owner. Mike gestured him to the back seat, and JC jumped in without hesitation, slamming the door.

"JC, I told you about this seat," said Mike. "When I drive, put this motherfucker back before I get it. Nigga got the seat all upright and shit," Mike said to no one in particular. "This is why I hate drivin' your car sometimes!"

JC's car smelled good and was so clean it might have passed for classy had I not noticed the porno magazine peeking out from under the passenger seat where I assumed Mike sat on the ride over. Mike and JC took vodka shots the whole way, which made me once more wish I had driven myself. By the time we got there, I figured they were both tipsy enough to make the most of whatever happened. It was a smart approach to the night and had me second-guessing my sobriety.

As we walked to the door, I stayed ten paces behind, as if the place was going to explode. They rang the doorbell. Feet pitter-patted toward it, and, after a moment, two rather large women answered the door and ushered Mike and JC inside.

I shuffled to the door, staring at the ground like a scared kid with a bad report card. As I walked inside, I saw the two girls more clearly.

"These are my boys, Roman, and JC," Mike told the two ladies.

"Hi, I'm Cassandra," the robust Caucasian girl said, greeting us with handshakes.

"And this is Michelle," she said, introducing us to her black, slightly less obese friend.

They were nothing to write home about, and definitely, nothing I would have ever touched. But Mike and JC didn't seem to have a problem with the girls' sizes, which made me feel a bit superficial.

"Where's your other friend?" Mike asked Cassandra.

"She's in her room. She gets in her little moods sometimes, but she should be out later."

"Looks like it's every man for himself," JC whispered to Mike, and he walked over and began flirting with Michelle.

I could tell Mike and Cassandra had formed a rapport before meeting today, and JC and Michelle seemed to be heading down the same path. I was left to fend for myself while they laughed, drank, and got to know each other better.

After about twenty minutes of neglect, Cassandra looked at me and decided she had better go see what was up with Victoria, who was unofficially my date for the night. She took so long that Michelle soon followed.

"I'm about to hit that," Mike boasted. He and JC slapped hands.

"Yeah, me, too," JC unconvincingly spouted.

"You better jump on her friend," JC said to me, like he were giving me a "can't miss" insider stock tip.

"That's if she ever comes out of her room," Mike said sarcastically. He and JC shared a laugh.

"If she looks anything like the two linebackers sitting out here, I'm good," I said, again feeling superficial.

"They can be as big as they wanna be, but when I'm actually *in* somethin', and you're wishin' you was me, we'll see who has the last laugh," Mike quietly countered as the girls walked back into the living room.

"She was on the phone with her parents," Michelle announced, reclaiming her seat beside JC.

"She'll be out in a minute," Cassandra added in my direction as she also sat back down.

They continued their conversations—laughing, giggling, flirting, and drinking—while I sat alone with my thoughts. Five minutes later, I heard a door open, followed by quiet steps towards the living room. I looked up and saw a beautiful woman standing in front of me. Light reflected off her face as though an angel had entered the room. Her long, silky hair was pulled into a ponytail, and her eyes were greener than envy. She was wearing pajama bottoms and a "wife beater," but she still looked more tempting than a well-dressed career woman.

"Vicki!" Cassandra got up. "Guys, this is Victoria. Vicki, this is JC, Mike, and Roman," she said, pointing at each of us. "Roman's visiting from Houston."

"Hello," Vicki said gently, waving at the three of us. JC and Mike rose to their feet, as though royalty had entered the room, and came over for a closer view. They were having impure thoughts as they shook her hand and stared into her eyes. Michelle and Cassandra were getting jealous and wanted the attention back on them. Cassandra told Victoria to take a seat. They went back to their original positions on the couch, with Victoria sitting beside me.

JC and Mike sneaked peaks at her, wishing they could trade seats with me, but neither her beauty nor the scent of her body wash put me in a social mood. I continued to look uncomfortable, and she did the same. Everybody else was engaged in conversation, with Mike and JC peering at Victoria every so often.

Taking it upon herself to be the consummate hostess, Cassandra blurted to Victoria, "Did I tell you Roman was visiting from Texas?"

"Uh, you told me before. Remember?" Victoria said, and then shot me an uncomfortable smile.

"Roman, Victoria just graduated in December. Now she's working as a loan officer at a bank," Cassandra informed me. Victoria gave her an annoyed look.

"Oh, yeah?" I asked. "What's your degree in?"

"Business management," she replied.

"That's a good field" I said, slipping back into silence.

The others continued gabbing while Victoria and I sat there like two uncomfortable mimes.

Mike and JC suggested Cassandra and Michelle give them a tour of the house. The girls giggled and led them from the room, leaving me alone with Victoria. I eased away, not wanting her to feel I was getting fresh.

Seconds ticked like minutes as silence consumed the room. I finally decided to cut the tension.

"You don't have to sit here with me. I promise I won't steal anything," I told her.

"It's okay. If I were you, I wouldn't want to be left alone in some stranger's house."

"No, really, don't worry about it. I'm sure you have better things to do than baby-sit strange guys."

"You're not that strange—well, not when compared to some of the guys who have come through here," she said, smiling. "You might actually be shyer than I am, and believe me—that is rare."

"I'm not used to meeting people under these circumstances. Don't take this the wrong way, but I don't meet people over talk lines, or whatever they're called, like my boys," I informed her. "I only came because they begged me, and I didn't really have anything better to do."

"I know what you mean. They've brought over a few guys before, and I can honestly say that this is the first time I've ever asked anything other than 'when are you leaving?'" We chuckled, and she continued. "Most of the guys are horny, perverted assholes. Can you believe the last time they brought guys over one followed me into my room and tried to kiss me."

"What ended up happening with that?"

"You mean besides him becoming Michelle's boyfriend?" She gave a slight smile.

I nodded.

"I ran into the bathroom while Michelle and Cassandra threw him out. I keep telling them it's dangerous inviting people they don't know over, especially ones they meet on a chat line."

"So why do they keep doing it?"

"They told me they like the excitement—seeing what the guys look like—kind of like a man lottery, I guess."

Lottery was right. *I* figured it was because they were big as houses, and over the phone, they could tell men they were one hundred and twenty-five pound beauties. I didn't want to press the issue of her reckless roommates more than I already had. Hell, if they didn't care, neither did I. As long as I got home safe and didn't have to go through another fiasco, as I had with the strippers, I was good.

Victoria was not only beautiful; she had ambition and goals. She talked about her work and her plans for the future.

"Roman, you awake?" Victoria said, waving her hand in my face.

"Yeah I'm here," I smiled. She was special.

"Thought I lost you for a second. I hope I'm not boring you," she said in a more serious tone.

"Oh, no, I was thinking about a couple errands I have to run tomorrow," I lied.

"How many more of these adventures do you think you're gonna go on with them?" she asked.

"This is the first and last, all, in one night. I'm not cut out for this. I like to meet women the traditional way."

"And how is that?" Victoria asked.

I laughed. "To tell you the truth, I have no clue. I haven't had a girlfriend in so long I might not even be straight any-more," I joked, as she giggled.

"Why haven't you had a girlfriend in so long? You seem like a nice enough guy. A poor selector of friends, maybe, but a good guy, nonetheless."

"It's not a very complicated story. I don't go out, I don't meet new people; I just go to work, come home, and sit on my butt. I think they call it being socially inept." I was only half-joking.

"No, you're not." Her voice was emphatic. "You have a lot going for yourself. You went to college, which is an accomplishment. You moved away on your own, which shows courage. You have a job, which shows you probably don't live with your mama," she said, giggling. "But seriously, even though things may not be perfect, they will get better. At least you're not running around, getting into trouble like some guys out there."

"What about you?" I asked.

"What about me?"

"I bet you've got like ten or twenty sugar daddies chasing after you."

“Not quite,” she said modestly. “I’m sure every woman has men chasing them, but it’s never the kind of guy I would want to bring home. They’ve either got too many strikes, kids, or women—and I’m just not into that.”

As our conversation continued, we heard strange sounds coming from Cassandra’s room. The way it kept slowing down and speeding up, I thought there was a lottery being held in her room. I imagined Mike’s small frame on top of Cassandra’s bulk, then spent the next couple of minutes trying to get that image out of my head. Our conversation got less and less chatty as the noises increased. Then came the grunting and moaning, which sounded more like cavemen playing tennis. *Oh, God*, I thought, then heard an "Oh, God," come from the room. *This is not happening*.

After about ten uncomfortable minutes, I turned to Victoria. “How long have they been going at it?” I asked, hoping to relieve the tautness.

“I don’t know. I just wish it would stop,” she said, glancing at the ceiling. “The thought of them together is going to give me nightmares for weeks.”

Eventually, Cassandra and Mike came out of the room, grinning. They looked disorganized and unkempt, which would have been a great indicator that they were fooling around had we not heard the evidence. Mike’s shirt was partly un-tucked and his mini-afro was matted on one side; Cassandra’s disheveled hair and braless chest made her look like an overweight hippie. If they were trying to disguise what they had just done, they were doing a terrible job.

Cassandra sat down next to Victoria. “What have you guys been doin’?”

“Nothing like what you guys have been doing,” she responded. Red swept across Cassandra’s face. Mike sported a mischievous smile.

“Is JC still in the back with Michelle?” Mike asked as he straightened his hair and clothes.

“Yeah. Unless they both jumped out a window, they should still be back there,” I answered.

"Unlike some people, we haven't heard a peep out of them," Victoria said, taking another shot at Mike and Cassandra.

"Let's go check on 'em, then," Mike said, walking to Michelle's room as though it were his house. Cassandra followed. "He better be gettin' some ass," Mike whispered to me as we approached Michelle's door.

Boom-boom-boom! Mike pounded on the door.

"What the hell ya'll doing in there?" he shouted.

Seconds later, Michelle came to the door, fully clothed, with creases on the side of her head.

"What do you guys want?" she snapped at Mike and Cassandra. Victoria and I watched from behind.

"What ya'll doin' back here?" Mike repeated, trying to see around her.

"We chillin'," Michelle said, opening the door wider to show JC asleep on her bed.

"Wake his sleepy ass up," Mike yelled at Michelle. "I can't believe that nigga went to sleep," Mike steamed, apparently angry that JC's night hadn't gone as well as his.

"It's okay. He can sleep here if he's tired," Michelle kindly announced. She smiled softly in JC's direction, the way a mother might smile at her sleeping child.

"No, he can't. Unless you gonna take him home in the morning, he gotta go with us," Mike said sternly.

"I can take him home if you want," Michelle countered.

"Wake his ass up," Mike shouted, disregarding Michelle's offer.

Mike leaned over and shook JC, yelling for him to wake up.

JC rolled over, still half-asleep, trying to figure what the commotion was. Everyone except him noticed the large, damp circle under him. We looked at one another, nonverbally confirming what the stain was. Mike was the first to comment.

"Rome, please don't tell me this grown-ass man just pissed in this girl's bed," Mike said, covering his face.

I said nothing as Mike screamed, "JC, get your three-year-old, bed-wetting ass up!"

JC didn't seem to realize what he had done until he stood up and gravity took over. Michelle's sheets and JC's pants had already absorbed most of the pee, but some slowly dripped to the carpet.

"Ew," Michelle yelled. "You're dripping!" She grabbed a towel from the back of her door and threw it at him. "Put it underneath you!" she yelled at JC, who stood there with a puzzled look on his face.

I finally intervened, calming Mike down. Mike always treated JC like a little brother, and JC took his punishment. Mike wasn't much bigger than JC, but to JC, Mike must have been the size of Shaq. I told Mike to go to the living room, so he wouldn't make the situation worse that it was, and then told JC to roll up his urine-soaked pants.

"Where's the bathroom?" I asked Michelle, ushering JC to the hallway.

As JC stood in the bathroom awaiting instructions, I asked the girls if they had any old clothes that would fit him. I asked all three out of respect, but I knew only Cassandra and Michelle were big enough—maybe even too big—to fill such a request.

"I think I may have something," Cassandra said, walking back to her room.

I told JC to take off "whatever was wet," which happened to be everything, and closed the door behind him. Moments later, I peeked back into the bathroom to see him totally naked, like a child awaiting a bath.

"Get in the shower," I told JC, carefully gathering his damp clothes and putting them into a bag Michelle gave me.

Cassandra came back with black sweats and a v-neck shirt for JC to wear. While he showered, I apologized to the girls, telling them JC had "a condition" that flared up occasionally.

"It's called "Euro-mice-a-ty-sis," I fibbed, stealing a line from *Seinfeld*. "He can't help it."

Michelle was a lot calmer than before. She seemed genuinely concerned for JC, asking about his condition and if he would be okay. When I heard the shower stop running, I went back into the bathroom with the clothes in hand for JC to wear.

He slowly put them on without looking me in the eye. When he finally did look up, his face was bright red with embarrassment. “I’m so sorry, Rome. I don’t know how this happened.”

“Don’t worry about it, man; the girls aren’t even pis—I mean, mad about it.”

“And what about Mike?” He asked as his voice shook.

“Don’t worry about Mike. I’ll deal with him if he starts acting stupid again,” I assured him.

“I can’t believe this happened. One minute we were talking, and the next thing you know, I wake up with pee running down my leg,” JC said. “I wasn’t even dreaming about water or nothing like that.”

“Like I said, man, don’t sweat it. Let’s just get outta here so we can get this night over with.”

JC’s borrowed clothes were uber-baggy. Even with the drawstring tightened to capacity, he still had to hold his sweatpants with one hand to keep them from falling below his bare butt.

We walked into the living room, and as soon as he saw the girls, he began apologizing and pleading his case, most of his dialogue directed at Michelle.

I went to Mike and demanded that he “be cool,” and not cause a scene; he agreed.

“Well, ladies, this has been an interesting night to say the least,” Mike said, attempting to sound sophisticated. “I hope we can do it again. He widened his arms to Cassandra for a hug.

JC looked at Michelle for a similar goodbye, and to my surprise, she hugged him, his pee-drenched clothes bag still in his hand.

"All right, Victoria, it's been nice getting to know you, and I hope all goes well," I told her, extending my hand for a shake. She stepped around my hand and instead hugged me.

"Yeah, I had a good time, too. Matter of fact, we should do this again, if you don't mind. I'd like to know more about you." She smiled as she pulled her cell phone from the pockets of her pajamas.

"That'd be cool," I said as I saved my number in her phone. "Call me anytime," I told her as I handed it back.

"I just might do that," she said, cutting her eyes at me and glancing through her phone to make sure I had properly stored the number in it, much the way a guy does when he meets a girl he really wants to know.

I was excited about meeting Victoria. She was definitely a showstopper, the kind of girl you wondered how the guy with her got so damn lucky. The crazy thing was that she was the aggressor. A girl like that wanted me!

"You should have put them pissy-ass clothes in the trunk; don't nobody wanna to smell that shit," Mike scolded JC from the front seat.

"Mike, it's his car, and it's not like you haven't been in that situation before," I reminded him. "Remember that party when you had too much to drink and it was coming out of both ends in my bathroom? I cleaned up after you and kept it between us, so how you gonna keep messin' with JC when you're no better than he is?"

"The difference is I was at your house. I wasn't in some female's bed, curled up like a lil' ass kid," Mike said. "And if you would have been pluggin' her, you wouldn't have had to worry about pissin' your pants!" The last was hurled at JC like a weapon.

"Whatever!" JC said, sounding like he was on the verge of tears. "My bad! Damn, can't you just drop it and leave me alone?"

"I just can't believe you, man," Mike said, chuckling. "A grown-ass man pissin' himself like a lil' ass boy. Am I gonna have to potty train your sorry ass? Goddamn, how do you live with yourself?" he asked, laughing harder than before.

Mike knew how to push JC's buttons, and this was one of those occasions when he was going to dial a long-distance number. Mike kept razzing him, and JC kept getting madder and madder. They were like siblings the way they communicated, or didn't, with one another.

JC finally had enough. He smacked Mike in the back of the head hard enough to knock it forward, causing him to swerve violently.

"Quit it, JC!" I yelled. "You're gonna make us crash."

"No, fuck him," JC shouted as he lunged at Mike. "I'm sick of his shit!"

Mike swerved again then regained enough control to hold the steering wheel in one hand and reach into the back seat to fend off JC with the other.

"What the fuck you doing, JC?" Mike roared, blindly swinging behind him as if a swarm of bees was attacking him.

"Pull over!" I yelled, also trying to control the wheel with one hand and keep JC off Mike with the other.

After what seemed an eternity, Mike pulled over. He and JC continued to go at one another while still in the car. I tried to break them up as they swung and swiped at one another in the little bit of space they had, but they weren't listening to my demands. I finally tired of trying to mediate their silly feud, and reached in the back seat and picked up JC's soiled clothing. Without thinking, I made my thumb and index finger into a pair of tongs and flung his piss-soaked pants at Mike, and then did the same to JC with his drenched underwear. They stopped when the splash of urine, followed by the smell, hit them.

"What the fuck?" Mike yelled at me—spitting and wiping where the soggy pants had touched his lips.

"What you do that for, Rome? I just took those clothes off," JC moaned.

"'Cause you guys are acting like a couple of girls, for real!" I barked at them. "Mike, I told you to leave JC alone, but no, you gotta push his buttons. And JC, if there were more cars on the road right now, we'd all be dead. That was some real stupid shit. If you wanna kill yourself, do it when I'm not in the car, all right? I'm tired, and I wanna go home; it's that simple. So you guys can either keep fighting, and I'll pick you up tomorrow morning, or we can all go home right now as homeboys—y'all decide quick, 'cause I got the keys right here," I said, and jiggled them for effect.

They said nothing and quietly got back into the car. It was weird, but they needed me, as a basketball team needs a coach, or an office needs a supervisor. They probably would have killed each other if I wasn't there, and knowing I was of use to someone, hell, anyone--made me feel good.

7

Gotta Leigh've Her Alone

The next morning, I woke to the sound of my cell phone ringing. I searched the room and found it just as it was going to voice mail.

"Hey, Roman, it's Leigh, long time no hear." I chuckled to myself thinking *In what world is not even a day a long time?* "I've been hanging out at my parent's house 'recovering,' as bored as can be. I figured I had better get a hold of you early, before you start your day. I was hoping we could hang out today because I don't think I can take watching soap operas and judge shows all day again—especially by myself. So when you get this message, give me a call, K? Bye."

I tried to roll over and go back to sleep, but that was out of the question. As much as I tried not to be, I was excited Leigh wanted to hang out. I was on a roll, and while I didn't like thinking about Leigh in a sexual manner, it was always nice to know I was attractive to the opposite sex.

For the next couple of minutes, I found myself smiling at the thought of what the day had to offer. Date-like activities like rollerblading and picnics were out of the question, but we had plenty of options. I wasn't sure what we were going to do, but I did know I'd be with Leigh, so the day would at least be interesting.

I usually hated mornings, but I was up, bright-eyed and bushy-tailed, after she called. It was as if I had drunk a two-liter of Mountain Dew and chased it with Red Bull. After washing up and reading the newspaper (borrowed from one of my out-of-town neighbors), I figured it was time to call Leigh back.

"What's up? How's your shoulder doing?" I asked.

"It's okay. It doesn't hurt or anything. My mom wants me to wear the sling, but I told her that my arm was okay and it wasn't necessary. Plus, I don't want everybody asking about it. My relatives have been calling, asking me all these questions, and wondering if I'm okay. I'm sick of talking about my accident. The same story over and over. I feel like a broken record."

"I can imagine, but the good thing is that you're getting better. I guess the time away from school is doing you some good," I told her.

I guess she thought I was trying to weasel out of us getting together because she said, "It's my shoulder, not my legs. I need to get out of this house. I'm tired of being home alone all day. I'm bored out of my mind! I can rest at home in LA if I'm going to be by myself all the time. Someone will come home during their lunch break and see if I need something, like coming home for fifteen minutes a day is helping! They wouldn't mind if you came and got me. So what time are you gonna be here?"

"Soon. Like maybe an hour or something. What do you wanna do, anyway?" I asked, hoping she had better ideas than the ones I had.

"How about breakfast?" she asked. "The only thing they have here is old people food."

"All right, that sounds good, 'cause I haven't eaten yet, either."

I got to her house forty minutes later, slightly nervous and trying to convince myself this was not a date. She opened the door not fully dressed, and invited me inside.

"You're early," she declared as I took a seat on the couch.

"I'll be ready in a few minutes," she yelled, shuffling upstairs. "Make yourself at home; the remote's on the table, and there are rice cakes in the fridge if you get hungry," she shouted with a laugh.

As I sat there flipping through channels, a dog small enough to be mistaken for a cat jumped into my lap. He wagged his tail and yapped as he tried to lick my face.

"Whose rat dog is this?" I yelled to Leigh.

"He's not a rat! He's a good dog," she said, coming down stairs as she fiddled with her hair. "This is Bruno, we just him back from the vet this morning," she said, bending over about an inch from the dog's nose. Bruno wagged his tail violently and tried to lick her face.

"Don't you know those beasts lick their own butts?" I said after the dog sneaked in a lick.

"No, he doesn't," she said, holding Bruno close to her face. "Bruno is part of the family, and for the record, dog saliva is supposed to be a hundred times cleaner than human saliva."

"I'm sure it is. Cause, humans are known for licking their butts and not brushing their teeth."

"Bruno is the cleanest-weanest little puppy-wuppy there ever was," she said in an annoying baby voice. "Here, smell him!" she said, putting him in my face as he eagerly licked me.

"Ahh -that's sick," I shouted, running to the bathroom to wash the salvia from my face.

The dog's spit didn't bother me as much as I let on. I just liked the attention I was getting from Leigh. I also really liked the way she played and giggled with her dog. Women must feel that way when they're around a man who's respectful of his mother, or able to entertain a young child.

"I'm leaving you here," I joked, grabbing my keys and walking to the door.

Leigh sprinted in front of me and put her back to the door, stopping me from opening it. I reached for the handle, and she sashayed her hips, blocking my hand. I tried again, with the same result.

"Move!" I yelled, trying to get by her.

"Uh-uh. You're not leaving without me."

She began to tickle me while standing in front of the door. Following her lead, I grabbed her by the waist and began tickling her; she giggled and knocked my hands away. I pretended to be frustrated as she trapped me. I avoided stepping on her yapping dog, grabbed her waist, and lifted her off the ground—she kicked as if I were abducting her—and moved her to the side to open the door. She crumbled to the ground, hissing as she grabbed her shoulder. As soon as I walked back to see if she was okay, she grabbed the keys out of my hand and slammed the door closed, trapping me once again.

"If you want your keys back, you're gonna have to get them!" She stuffed them inside her collared black shirt.

"You win. Let's just go," I said, extending my hand for the keys.

"No giving up! If you want your keys, come and get 'em," she challenged.

Knowing there wasn't much I could do without my keys I walked towards her and demanded them.

"Close your eyes!" Leigh said, as though she had a big surprise for me.

"No, I don't want you putting that mangy beast in my face again. Just hand over the keys, and we'll be okay."

"Close your eyes," she said again. "I put them in my shirt, and you have to close your eyes if you want them back."

Just go in the bathroom and get 'em out, I thought to myself as I closed my eyes, reluctantly playing Leigh's game.

"Okay, you can open them," she said, standing face to face with me, passion in her eyes.

I was silent and motionless. “Why are you so close?” I asked. My body trembled, and waves of heat rose from the top of my head.

“Why are *you* so close?” she seductively fired back.

“I was standing here first,” I told her, taking a step back, suddenly knowing how Superman felt in the presence of kryptonite.

“Now I’m standing here,” she said, stepping forward to invade my personal space again.

I didn’t know what to do. I wanted her with every fiber of my being, but this was Leigh, Nikki’s sister—the same Leigh who used to tattle on her sister for talking to boys on the phone. This was getting old. I was sick of being in compromising positions and having to pull away.

“I can’t do this,” I whispered, closing my eyes to make her beauty less of a factor.

“Do what?” She sounded as if she’d stepped closer.

“This,” I said, gathering strength to break the spell she had over me.

“Can I have my keys now?” I asked.

“Here,” she said, reaching into her blouse and handing them to me.

“Are you ready to go?” I asked.

“Not yet.” She sounded discouraged as she walked upstairs.

I was officially afraid to be alone with her. I had been naive about her line of questioning before, but now I knew she had feelings for me. I decided that from then on, I would do what I could to keep from being in awkward situations with her. I simply would not be able to stand up to her if she cornered me again.

“Where do you want to eat?” I asked as we got into the car.

“I don’t care, just as long as it’s not made of wheat, oats, bran, or soy,” she said with a slight smile.

As we drove I expected her to be in a sour mood, the same mood she was in a couple of days ago when I wasn’t answering her questions. But no, she actually seemed pretty normal, which again left me guessing.

I couldn't figure her out. She might as well have been a Rubic's Cube the way she had me guessing. I was fed up with her and her constant ups and downs. She acted as though she was on Valium, or other anti-depression medication. It was time to go back to being friends who saw each other every couple of years or so. Anything had to be better than our "Bobby and Whitney" relationship—especially since we weren't in a relationship.

"Look, Leigh," I said, turning down the radio. "What's going on with you? You've been at my throat more the last couple of days than any woman I've ever dated—and we're not dating!" She glanced at me. I continued. "The reason I came back was you. I'm serious, Leigh," I said, concentrating on her more than the road. "If I've done or said something that's upset you, let me know. Anything's better than walking on eggshells when I'm around you. I don't know which side of you I'm going to get."

Much to my dismay, she didn't respond, but sat there and said nothing, staring out the window as though she were seeing San Diego for the first time.

"Leigh," I said in a monotone voice. "Leigh, say something—anything—please!"

Although I begged for a response, it seemed she didn't want to give me one. I wanted an answer of any kind. Good or bad—it didn't matter.

I pulled the car over and shut off the engine.

"Leigh, I'm not leaving this spot until you tell me what's going on with you," I told her.

The clang of the keys consumed the silence, like wind chimes on a breezy day. Her face was still glued to the window, so I tapped her shoulder for an answer. I got out of the car and walked to the passenger side to catch a glimpse of her face, which had eluded me for the last couple minutes.

As soon as I got to her side, she turned her face again. I felt like she was the neighbor on *Home Improvement,* what with the way she outmaneuvered me every time I tried to scan her face.

I should just grab her damn arm, I thought to myself, but I knew wasn't the type of guy to get physical with a woman—especially one this emotional.

"You know what? Forget this," I exclaimed, just barely stopping myself from shouting a frustrated F-bomb. "I've had enough," I rambled, reaching for the keys, which had fallen beside the center console. "I have no idea what you want and I'm not going to sit here all day waiting for you to tell me." I started the engine and aggressively shifted into drive.

I was ready to speed away and try to forget any of this had just happened, when Leigh turned around, tears dripping from her eyes.

"You wanna know what I want?" she yelled with a sniffle.

I didn't answer; I just sat there, figuring I had done enough investigating for one day. I tried to keep my eyes forward while waiting for her to finish.

"I want you!" she shouted, staring so deeply into my eyes that she could have seen my every thought.

She took a deep breath and continued. "I've always wanted you," she said, with the honesty of a child. "It's been you from day one. I've loved you since I was fourteen years old, Roman."

I must have looked stunned. She kept talking.

"I thought if I ever had a chance to go after you, I would do it with all my heart. It wasn't a schoolgirl crush, either. You were it for me. When you left, I was so disappointed—not just at you, but at the possibility of us. I thought I had gotten over you, but when you came to see me in the hospital, I was fourteen years old, all over again. You may not have known it, but you never left my heart, Roman. Never!"

Her revelation caught me off guard. I was speechless. What was I supposed to say after such a heartfelt admission?

"Really?" That was the best I could do, and she was lucky to get that after a disclosure of this magnitude.

"Didn't you wonder why you were the only one of Nikki's friends I ever invited to my parties or soccer games? God, I would have invited you to a funeral if it meant getting to spend time with you."

"No, not really," I admitted, hoping not to sound too crass. "I mean, I knew you liked having me around sometimes, but that's about all the thought I put into it. You were so young back then, so I wasn't thinking about you like that."

"Well, you were special to me," she said, dropping her head as though her speech had taken all of her energy.

I had never been put in this position by any woman, let alone a woman I cared about. Again, I was left without words. Hell, what was I supposed to say? *I love you, too.* Maybe if she was my girlfriend—but she wasn't, and I damn sure wasn't her boyfriend. This was little Leigh. Well, maybe not so little anymore, but it's hard to envision someone you've watched grow up as anything other than a smiley-faced kid.

"Leigh, I don't know what to say. I mean, I guess I'm flattered and all, but—"

"I know," she said, cutting me off mid-sentence. "I'm too young, or I'm just like a little sister. Tell me," she said, forgetting she had just cut me off.

"Well, yeah," I responded. "You are young, and you are just like a sister to me—and did you forget that you also have a boyfriend? Remember the traveling salesman, or whatever he does?" I said. "Or did you forget about him?"

"No, I didn't forget about him. Things with him are complicated, and I'm going to leave it at that. And as far as being too young, you know, Roman, too young is a man in China," she said sounding like she had been watching way too many rap videos. "You're only twenty-five, Roman. Yeah, you're right—with that huge four-year gap, what could we possibly have in common? That whole big brother thing is just an excuse, and a lame one at that. I never looked at you as my big brother and neither did anyone else! My parents barely even remember you, so how are you going to be my big brother?"

I didn't believe she felt that way. If I wasn't like her big brother, then what was I? I knew she was talking mostly out of frustration, so I tried my best to ignore her blasphemous comments.

"It may not be weird for you, Leigh, but it would for me," I told her. "I've watched you grow from an annoying little girl into the woman I see before me now. And as much as you hate the big brother reference, that's what I've considered myself all these years."

She looked at me. I took a deep breath and continued.

"Unlike a lot of guys out there, I care that you have a boyfriend. I respect you too much not to, and I'm shocked that that doesn't mean more to you." I sounded like the good guy on a talk who receives a standing ovation for agreeing to care for a child that isn't his.

"You don't understand," she mumbled, trying to control her tears. "You just don't get it."

As we sat there trying to figure out where all of this was heading, she looked at me with tear-drenched eyes. "Just take me home, Roman," she whimpered.

"I thought we were gonna have breakfast," I said, even though I understood her not wanting to eat. For the most part, neither did I. It had been an emotional morning—even for me.

"I'm not hungry anymore," she stated, which came as no surprise.

"So you just want me to take you home?" I asked.

"Yes, please," she said, turning her head to watch the traffic.

I couldn't have predicted this was going to happen, but I still felt responsible. Most people would have jumped at an opportunity to be with Leigh. "*Who the hell does he think he is*?" I imagined everyone saying. She was young *and* had a boyfriend, I reassured myself. *But she's also beautiful, and I do care for her,* another voice pointed out.

You did the right thing, I assured myself one last time, going over it again as we drove away.

8

BBQ'd Truth's

Just as I was feeling good about the situation with Leigh, I got a call from Mike.

He started his conversation with, "Let's go get some butt-naked hoes, dog!"

"What?" I spewed. He slowly repeated his demand.

"I said, 'let's-go-get-some-butt-naked-hoes.'"

"Mike, why are you calling me so early with this nonsense? Don't you have to go to work?" I asked, wondering when and where he was planning to get these so-called "hoes."

"I'm already at work," he said with a chuckle. "But later on I wanna get with you—and, oh, yeah—can I use your house? I got a surprise lined up for you later."

"What's the surprise?" I asked as if I knew I nothing of the meaning of surprise.

"Just leave a key for me under the mat. You won't be disappointed," he said, sounding as sure a Las Vegas gambler.

"All right, man, I'm gonna trust you, but I don't want any bald-headed, transvestite midgets running around my house. And do not use my bed for anything—not even sleep," I warned him.

“Aw, it’s like that?” Mike yelled into the phone.

“Yep, it’s like that. The last time you used my bed, my sheets were all spotted and stiff. Just stay fully clothed and don't go in my room”

“Whatever. Just trust me, man. You’re gonna like this surprise.”

Any other time I would have put up more of an argument—not that I would have said no, but I would have asked more questions. However, my mind was more focused on Leigh and how to smooth things over with her. As long as Mike wasn’t doing anything too freaky, to the point where I'd have to burn my bed, I was cool.

After the Leigh fiasco, I had nothing to do. Like Leigh, most everybody I knew was either working or busy. My father was still on my back about us spending time together, and while hanging out with him wasn’t tops on my list of pastimes, I decided to get it over with sooner, rather than later.

I called my dad, and he told me that he was busy, but all too happy to make time for us to have lunch and “catch up.”

He came over, picked me up, and took me to one of his favorite restaurants—Nino’s Barbeque Warehouse, where twenty bucks guaranteed enough meat to clog an artery. My father and I didn’t get along, but Nino’s made him a lot more bearable.

He genuinely loved the place, and it was refreshing to see his face light up as each overly sauced rib approached his awaiting palate. For the first time in years, I was enjoying an outing with my father. He didn’t seem like the man I resented more and more with each passing day. Today, he was the cool, funny, witty, charming man I could see my mother, or any woman for that matter, falling for.

“Roman,” my father started, “I think that girl is looking at you. Matter of fact, I’m sure she’s looking at you.” He casually fished inside his mouth for the carcass lodged between his teeth.

"Where?" I asked, looking around.

"Behind you—about seven o'clock," he said, as if he had been in the military. "But don't look yet. She's still looking over. Okay, now look! See her? The one in the red shirt. She's not bad, either," he said, with a look of approval.

I turned around to see my admirer; she looked very familiar, almost like…

"Dad, I think that's Tina."

"Tina who?"

"Tina Lampe, the girl I used to date in high school," I told him.

"You used to date her? Go over and say hi then. She's been looking at you the whole time we've been here," he informed me.

"I'm not going to say hi to her! That's the girl who dumped me for another girl in the middle of PE class." I looked at her to be sure. "Yeah, that's her."

He stopped chewing. "Well, you don't have to go over there, because I think she's coming over here," he said.

"For real?" I exclaimed, wiping the mess off my face, not sure I was ready to face my past.

I made a ninety-degree turn, and there she was in front of me, big as day and real as ever. She still had her signature pretty face. Her almond skin could have decorated a bowl of rocky road ice cream quite nicely.

"Hi, Roman," she gleefully said, holding the hand of a boy no older than five.

"Hey, how you doing?" I returned, making sure my greasy lips were dry.

"I'm good, you know. Just being a mom and—Ricky, get yo' ass away from there," she yelled to another little boy, and then turned back to me as if nothing had happened. "Yeah, I'm just taking care of my boys. What about you? I heard you were living in, like, Arkansas or something."

"Houston," I corrected, noticing a bulge in her stomach.

"Oh, really? So how long are you in town?" she asked.

"I don't know. I've been here three days so far, but I'm not sure when I'm going back."

"Hi," my father interrupted. "I'm Tony Sullivan - Roman's father."

"Hi, I'm Tina. Your son and I used to date back in high school."

I was amazed, as much as offended, that she was acting as if she hadn't done me incredibly wrong back in high school. Not that I wanted her to come out and admit, in front of my father and everybody in the restaurant, that she was a lying slut or anything, but come on. I was duped in front of an entire gym class by a girl who claimed to be a lesbian, who was now standing in front of me with at least two kids, and possibly a third on the way.

"Are all these your kids?" I asked out of spite, hoping they ran her ragged every day.

"Yeah," she said, looking back at the older boy to see if he was getting into more mischief. "I have another one on the way," she informed me, rubbing her bulbous belly.

"Really? Well, congratulations. When are you due?" I asked, pretending to care.

"I'm almost two months now. It's supposed to be due in early December, but the other two were premature, so I'm guessing' sometime in November."

"That's nice." I gave her a fake smile. "I hope everything goes well with you and your family."

"Yeah, you, too. Matter of fact, here's my number. I just recently became single again, so if you get a chance, you should definitely ring me up. We could do some catching up," she said with a sincere smile.

Was she serious? I thought to myself. Aloud I said, "Yeah, uh—sure, I'll give you a call."

"Cool. When you get some time," she said.

She hugged my father and I, wiped her little boy's nose, and strolled back to her table, with no mention of her past indiscretions. She put me through hell and back and had the audacity to ask me to give her a call. We laughed about it for a while, both astonished and impressed by her gall.

"So when are you gonna give her a call?" said my father, almost overcome by laughter. "Add you, mix, and you've got yourself a ready-made family," he said, laughing harder.

"You got jokes, huh?" I chuckled, in spite of myself. "To tell you the truth, I kind of want to go over and thank her. I was so head over heels for her back then, I would've done anything she asked. The day she dropped that bomb on me, I didn't think I would ever get over it. Seeing her today makes me feel a lot better. Plus, she's way too fertile," I said, and we shared another chuckle.

"Thank God I'm not one of her babies' daddies. I can hardly take care of myself right now," I said aloud, but to myself, thinking of how miserable a father I might be at the present time.

"Thank God is right," my father said, as I balled up her number and tossed it into a plate of devoured rib bones.

We had eaten so much barbeque I could have burped the alphabet. Just when I leaned back, surprised at how well the visit was going, my father's mood changed, and he decided he had to have a real conversation about the past—which was the root of most of my problems.

"Son, I'm sure you can understand me wanting to see you after all the time you've been away. I missed you a lot, and I put a lot of the blame on myself for you leaving the way you did."

You're goddamn right it's your fault, I thought to myself, letting him continue.

"But you've also got to know that I am human, and I do make mistakes. No one is perfect, son, and I'm a shining example of that. Your mother and I were going through a lot of problems back then. I'm not justifying what I did, but your mother and I knew our marriage wasn't working, and we no longer wanted a dysfunctional life."

"Mom never stopped loving you," I fired back. "You single-handedly tore our family apart. Not mom, not me—you! Damn! Dad, how could you do that to Mom? She would have done anything for you, and that was the thanks she got for twenty some-odd years of marriage!" I took a deep breath.

I felt like leaning over and smacking him. Then I wanted to run away and go back to my life of seclusion. A number of things I could do to cope with the pain of the situation my father had put my mother and I through flashed through my head. I finally straightened up; I wasn't going to run away. He was going to hear what I had to say to him.

"You want to talk to me, father to son, right?" I asked heatedly. Several on-lookers turned to see what the commotion was.

It was amazing how fast our conversation had gone from casual to confrontational, but this was the stickiest of situations—one that got my blood boiling quickly.

"Okay, let's talk then," I said, a scowl on my face. "I hate what you did, I have no respect for you, and I don't know if I ever will."

I felt myself gaining momentum. My heart pounded less from fear and more from confidence.

"I don't even know if I love you anymore. You fucked me up in ways you will never know," I said, wondering if I had crossed the line using the f-bomb in front of my father—something that I had never done. "I'm twenty-five years old, and I can't tell you how much life I've missed in the last three years. I can deal with that! What I can't deal with is what's happened to Mom. She's so up and down nowadays, I don't even know who she is anymore." I willed myself to take a deep breath.

"I left because I needed to find my own way, but instead, I found myself in a city I knew nothing about, surrounded by people whom I knew even less. And do you know what I've figured out? Nothing!" I rushed to say before he could respond.

I had caused a big enough scene for management to come towards our table. Before he reached our table, I got up and walked towards the exit. I had no idea where I was going, and I had no ride home, but I needed to get out of the restaurant and away from my father. A few moments later, he rushed out of the restaurant.

"Wait, son," he yelled in my direction. "Roman!"

With my eyes close to tears and a heart full of anger, I turned and looked at him. "How could you do that to Mom, and with her sister of all people? You always told me to treat women with respect, and you run off and have an affair with your wife's sister? And to make matters worse, you bring a child into the world with her!

"You know, Dad, I always wanted a little brother. I just never thought I would get one like this," I said sarcastically. "I guess you have to really watch what you wish for."

He was at a loss for words, but I had waited a long time to tell him how I felt, and I thought I deserved, at very least, an explanation.

"I'm sorry, son," he said. "That's all I can say. I'm sorry. I don't have any excuses for what I did. All I want you to know," he said, walking closer to me, "is that I never blamed you or your mother for anything; it was all on me. I love you, and believe it or not, I love your mother and always will. I was selfish, wrong, and only worried about myself. I went about it the wrong way, son, and I lost you and your mother because of it. But on the flip side, I have a young son now; I have to be the best father I can be and teach him not to make the same mistakes I did. I know it's hard to understand, but I am a different man now than I was then, and if you give me another chance, I will prove it to you."

We were silent. I tried not to make eye contact, as he tried to do exactly that. I was still angry, but letting loose three years of frustration lifted a huge weight off my shoulders.

"Dad, just take me home," I said, sounding just like Leigh earlier. "All I want from you is a ride home."

I knew he wanted resolution, but it was too early, and I was too disappointed to forgive him right then. He nodded in resignation and drove me home. Before I got completely out of range, he yelled, "Rome, you have a little brother now, and no matter how you feel about me, he's innocent in all this. He needs his big brother."

I stopped without turning around and thought of the little brother I had never seen. "What's his name?" I yelled, back still towards him.

"Mathew. Mathew Alexander," he shouted back.

9

Apologetic Apologies

After that heated exchange with my father, I didn't know what my next move would be. I thought about booking a flight back to Texas, but quickly abandoned that idea. I had unfinished business here. Visions of Leigh kept popping into my head. I wondered what she was doing, how she was feeling, and if she was thinking about me. Straightening things out with her was my only logical move.

"Hey, Roman," Mr. and Mrs. Scott said as they opened the door. "It's good to see you're still in town," Mrs. Scott said, grabbing a jacket as Mr. Scott sidled behind her to help her into it.

"We were just leaving, but Leigh is upstairs in her room. She has been in a bit of a mood since we came home, but you're free to go up and see what you can do with her."

I wanted to laugh. *See what you can do with her*. It sounded kind of sexual, but I was sure they hadn't recognized the undertones of her statement.

"It was nice to see you, Roman," she said. They made their way to the garage and took off in their expensive European sedan.

"Leigh, we need to talk about what happened earlier," I yelled, walking up the stairs. I knocked on her door. "I've always held you in high regard, and I was a little surprised at what happened earlier, especially since you have the whole boyfriend thing going on. Even if I didn't feel you were family, I would never do anything with any woman I knew was involved. That's just not me."

Nothing. No sound. I sighed and tried again.

"I really wish you would come out and talk to me face to face," I continued. "Leigh. Leigh!" I knocked some more. "Just talk to me for a minute, then I'll be out of your life forever, if that's you want."

Silence.

"You know what? Forget it. If you can't come out and talk to me like an adult, then I don't want to talk to you either," I exclaimed, as I headed back towards the stairs.

Suddenly, I heard a door open down the hall.

"Who's there?" I heard Leigh ask cautiously.

"It's me! Roman!" I raced back up the stairs towards the voice.

"What do you want?" she said, a hint of disgust in her voice.

"This is your room? I just finished spilling my guts to you—well, to the door, anyway. I thought your room was the first one on the right," I said, shaking my head in embarrassment.

"I was in my room napping and listening to music. That's probably why I didn't hear you," she said.

"Look, Leigh—" I stood straighter. "I came to tell you I'm sorry for all this. You know I would never intentionally hurt you. I wish we could go back to the way things were before this happened. I don't feel like burning any more bridges while I'm here, 'cause I've already done enough of that."

"I know what you mean. I apologize, too," she mouthed softly. "But I'm not sorry for telling you the way I feel. I meant every word of what I said, Roman. I figured if I didn't tell you now, then when? Who knows the next time I'll see you? I didn't want another three years to pass before I told you."

Turning Leigh down would have been easier had she been less attractive. Every time I looked in her eyes, I was overwhelmed; I treated her like Medusa, avoiding her gaze at all costs.

I tried to be tactful. "We've been though enough today, Leigh. I don't feel right going there with you. And as corny as it sounds, I respect you and your family way too much. If you were any other girl in this world, I would be all over you like a cheap suit, believe me; it's not like I have beautiful women coming at me every day."

The moment I finished, I felt like striking my words from the record. A rejection was a rejection; it didn't matter how I dressed it up.

"You think I'm beautiful?" she said, smiling and seemingly dismissing everything else I'd said. "I thought you were going to say it yesterday, but this is the first time you've officially said it," she beamed.

"Yeah, uh, well you know you're a pretty girl. I mean, yeah, you're pretty, but that doesn't change any of this, so don't get it twisted," I warned.

"It does, too, change things. If you're attracted to me, enjoy being with me, and like my personality, then the only thing keeping us apart is—what? You respecting me and my family too much?" She giggled.

I was shocked. I guess things worked differently for men than women. I'd had bunches of girls tell me I was cute, only to keep walking when I tried to talk to them.

"Come on, Roman, that can't be it. There must be something else. If that's the best you've got, that's really weak," she said.

"Okay, maybe that's not the best reason, but I have a few others. First, you're already involved, remember?" I said as her smile faded.

"I know that, but like I said before, you don't know the whole story."

"Well, tell me. I would love to hear it."

"Now's not the time, but I promise I'll tell you when the time's right," she said.

"When you tell me, I'll listen more seriously about the possibilities of you and I," I told her, happy to use that as an excuse. "But until then, Roman Sullivan is not getting involved with anybody else's woman. Do we have a deal?" I said, extending my hand.

"Okay, it's a deal," she agreed.

"Well, it's been real, but I gotta go. Mike's at my house, and I gotta make sure he doesn't tear it up. Think about what I said and let me know. I promise I won't leave until we've had that talk."

"What's the other reason?" she asked just as I had opened the door.

"The other reason for what?" I asked, one hand on the doorknob.

"The other reason we wouldn't work."

"Because, I live in Houston," I said before closing the door and leaving.

I wasn't in the mood for company, but I had already promised Mike the use of my house so he could entertain his guests and give me my surprise. I just hoped I would be able to relax, stay out of their way, and most importantly, keep my place from being destroyed.

When I walked in, I saw the exact three-some we'd visited a couple days ago. JC and Michelle were playfully touching each other, which shocked me, given what had happened the last time they were together.

Three on three means no sleep for me, I told myself in a Johnny Cochran-like manner, knowing Mike and JC expected me to keep Victoria company. As beautiful as she looked, I just wasn't in the entertaining mood. All day, I had envisioned an evening of television and relaxation, and there was no way that was going to happen with Victoria thrust upon me.

Selfishness won out as I greeted Mike, JC, and the ladies and proceeded to my room to begin my modest dream. As soon as I kicked off my shoes, Mike barged into my room like an upset parent.

"What the hell you doing, Rome? Why you in here by yourself when all of us is out there?" he asked.

"First of all, Mike, don't be busting' in my room like you're my dad. Second, I'm in here because I feel like being alone. What's wrong with that?"

"You saw Victoria, right?"

"Yeah, and?"

"Well, surprise—I invited her over for you and this is the thanks I get? You tellin' me you'd rather watch old episodes of *Full House* than be with her?"

Mike was trying to be slick, and while Victoria was a surprise, it benefitted him as well. While my surprise and I were hanging out, he would be getting a surprise from Cassandra later that evening, and trying to use my house for it. It was like buying someone a gift because you think you're going to get one in return.

"No, I'm not saying that. I just wanted to come home and relax. You asked if you could use my crib; you never said anything about me having to entertain anyone. I wouldn't care if it were Leigh, Victoria, or the Queen of Egypt; I don't want to be bothered right now. Is that all right with you?"

"Oh, I see. This is about Leigh," Mike said, convinced he had the situation figured out. "Okay, I'll take her home then," he said, walking out of my room, "but you should have just said that when I talked to you earlier."

Mike couldn't push my buttons the way he could JC's, but no matter how many times I tried to tell him one thing, he was going to believe what he wanted, especially when it came to Leigh, who ironically, he barely remembered.

I rushed to catch him before he reached the living room, and agreed to take Victoria off his hands. After washing up and throwing on a new shirt, I made my appearance.

I greeted Michelle and Cassandra before going to Victoria for a long overdue hug. "Sorry about earlier," I whispered in her ear. "I was just shocked to see you guys, plus a little bit tired."

She brushed it off and smiled sincerely. "Don't worry about it. I get the same way sometimes." I thought about the first time we met and knew she meant it.

Three minutes into the conversation, Victoria again impressed me. In that short time, she'd convinced me to find out all I could about her.

We had separate conversations going simultaneously, reminding me of a high school cafeteria. After a half-hour of talking amongst ourselves, Mike jumped up.

"You guys wanna go hot-tubbing?" he blurted. "I have a friend who works security at a hotel. It has a super-tight hot tub we can use after ten, when it closes. We'll be the only ones there," he threw in, making it sound more intimate.

It must have been the enthusiasm in his voice because we all went along with the idea. Mike must have had it planned because everybody was prepared for the possibility of a late night swim. I was going to volunteer to drive but before I could the four of them packed themselves into Cassandra's economy-sized Hyundai, as though they were double dating on an episode of *Andy Griffith*.

When Victoria got into my car, I knew she was impressed. The leather seats hugged her curvaceous body like a personalized glove, and the jet-black interior and the soulful crooning of Anthony Hamilton could have made a lesbian change her ways. Victoria leaned back, looked ahead, and uttered a cool "nice car," without once breaking her poise.

The hotel's pool area was as nice as advertised. It had an Olympic-sized pool and a Jacuzzi big enough for all of us—which was either going to be really good or bad. Cassandra wore an over-sized white shirt with checkered shorts, while Michelle sported a pair of gray spandex shorts with a number ninety-three Jovan Kearse Tennessee Titans jersey. Both combinations were terribly unflattering. Had it been sunny, everyone would have wanted to lie next to them for their natural sun-shielding abilities.

Victoria, on the other hand, had on a devastating bathing suit. Everything on her body was perfectly placed and pronounced; she made me drool like a starving dog every time I glanced in her direction.

After frolicking in the hot tub and a couple of laps around the pool, Victoria seemed bored and suggested we head elsewhere. We put our clothes back on and headed for the beach, not letting our friends know we were leaving.

She immediately left me behind to put her feet in the calm seawater. Playfully splashing me, she ran in the calf high water like an uninhibited child. After a couple of moments, she smiled, demanding I join her.

"It's way too cold to be in the water." I shuddered at the thought.

"The water's warmer at night." She grinned and kicked water my way.

"If my feet are cold, so is the rest of my body," I said, fleeing from an approaching tide.

"Oh, come in. I promise it's not that cold."

I decided to ignore my shivering body and hardened nipples, and take a "leap of faith" into the chilly sea.

"Ahh!" I yelled like a commando in the jungles of South America, trying to deflect the thought of the bitter ocean water hitting me. However, just before reaching the water, I tripped on a clump of seaweed and fell face first into the sand. My head was stuck in the ground like a frightened ostrich, and the ocean water soaked my body anyway. Victoria was right—the water wasn't cold at all. The bad news? I was drenched, covered in sand, and more embarrassed than a priest caught in a strip club.

Victoria helped me up. I wiped my face and shook my head in disgrace. She asked if I was okay and I chuckled, which turned into a laughing hysteria once she knew I was fine.

After the ultimate icebreaker, we sat side by side, watching the waves crash against the shore. I hoped the seawater would have a calming effect on me, as my heart was pounding a mile a minute. Victoria stared at the ocean, her hair blowing lightly in the wind. She smiled, off in her own peaceful world. I wanted to say something, but couldn't—the lump in my throat was too huge. The last thing I wanted was distract her from the waves. I just sat with her, looking into the ocean, trying to find the same peace and comfort that seemed to possess her body.

"Don't you just love the ocean?" she sighed, looking as though she had just returned from a day spa. "It's so refreshing. I could come here every day. All my stress and problems get washed away with each wave."

Surprised, I asked, "What kinds of problems could you possibly have?"

I had no idea why I said that, I guess I was at a loss for words and trying to come up with something that at least sounded decent. I felt a lot like the girlfriend who knows nothing about sports, and wants to impress her boyfriend, but gets a homerun confused with a touchdown.

"What do you mean?" she replied, taking her gaze off the water.

"You said it's like the water washes away your stress and problems. I was just wondering what kind of problems you have. I mean, I know everyone has problems, but you seem like you would have less."

She watched me as I fumbled for words. "I mean, not less, but you know what I mean. You're too good. I mean—"

I stopped mid-sentence, hoping I hadn't insulted Victoria with my rambling. "I'm just going to shut up," I said, unable to explain why, out of the six billion human beings on earth, she was the only one who didn't have problems.

"Don't shut up," she said, smiling. "I'm flattered that I look like I'm above having problems. Unfortunately, I do—just like anyone else. If it makes any difference, I wish I didn't," she said, cutting her eyes at me.

Victoria had a certain appeal that drew me to her like a moth to light. I couldn't resist being around her and wondered how I ever thought watching television could compare to an evening with her.

"What are some of your problems?" I asked, feeling more confident and comfortable with every passing minute. "And for the record, I know everyone has problems; it's just that some have more than others."

"What are some of yours," she asked, "since I look like I don't have any?"

"I asked you first."

"Tell me something private, and I will return the favor."

It must have been the misty air or the lure of the moon, maybe even the glow from Victoria's face or her easy-going nature, but I felt like I could talk to her.

"Okay, I'll bite," I said. "I moved to Houston to get away from my family and haven't really spoken to anybody from San Diego in about three years. How's that?"

"Really?" she said, intrigued by the taste of gossip I had given her. "Not to be nosey, but what happened with you and your family? I mean, three years is a long time."

I took a deep breath. "It's a long story, but I will tell you this—if what happened to me had happened to you, you would have moved away, too."

"Okay, I'll accept that."

"What about you?" I asked, as she gazed into the choppy water.

"Look!" she blurted, running closer to the restless waves.

"At what?" I asked. What was so important that I couldn't get an answer to my question?

"Look at that!" she said, gazing even deeper into the water than before. I copied her squat.

"What am I supposed to see?" I asked, feeling as though I were looking at a piece of 3-D art.

"It's red tide," she said joyously.

"Red who?" I asked, ignorant to her point of interest.

"Red tide," she said, stepping into the tide line. "It's early this year."

"I have no idea—before I could finish, she shushed me and waved me over.

"Red tides are caused by runoff from pollution, and make the waves glow. It looks like someone's shining a light on them. Look, there goes one. Look, right there," she shouted, corkscrewing my body. "You see it? Look how the waves glow! Look, there's another one!" she yelled, still holding onto me.

After she eased her grip, I began to see what she meant. The progression of waves marching on the shore was gorgeous. One wave would crash, the water would calm, and the next took its place.

"That is pretty cool," I remarked. "How'd you find out about this? On the Discovery Channel?" I joked, still focusing on the water.

"No, not the Discovery Channel," she said sounding slightly offended. "You asked what kind of problems I have. In college, I wanted to be either a biologist or an oceanographer—something dealing with the earth; that was what I always dreamed about as a kid. I wanted to major in some type of life science, but my parents decided that going into business was best for me. I couldn't really argue because they were the ones paying for my education."

She stared out at the horizon. "Don't get me wrong. I love my parents and all, but I wish they understood how much I wanted to be a scientist—working outside and seeing what makes the world what it is; I couldn't imagine a better job than that."

"Why didn't you tell them?" I asked.

"You don't know my parents. They're both very successful business people. According to them, work should translate into financial gain. They want me to have a big house and a Mercedes, like them. They don't understand that I don't care about that. I couldn't care less about a Mercedes, Roman, and if I made twenty thousand dollars a year doing something I loved, I'd be happy! The funny thing is they've been divorced almost ten years, but I have never met two people more alike than they are. I guess opposites attract only so much." A tear began to form in the corner of her eye.

I wanted to ask why she didn't just take out loans and pay for school herself, but she was close to breaking down and doing her best not to cry. I eased down beside her, she rested her head on my shoulder, and we sat silently for what seemed like forever, gazing into the sea.

"Rome!" a voice yelled, startling Victoria and I out of our beachfront daydream.

"Where the hell ya'll been? We been callin' ya'll for the last hour tryin' to find you."

"We've been right here," I explained through a muffled yawn.

"Ya'll been sittin' here for two hours? Goddamn, I could've got some trim if it wasn't for this cake-ass nigga," Mike said, pulling out his cell phone, seemingly unconcerned if Victoria heard him or not.

"Cassandra, I found 'em. They was having a romantic evening on the beach, just like you thought," Mike said. He looked at Victoria and handed her his phone. "She wanna talk to you."

As Victoria explained to Cassandra that she left her phone in my car and was perfectly fine, Mike strutted in my direction with a devilish grin on his face.

"You tryin' to hit that?" Mike said, confusing me as to whether he was asking or telling.

"What?"

"You tryin' to hit that, huh?" he said again, in the same perplexed tone. "This fool is really tryin' to chop that," Mike said, his head up as though talking to the Gods.

"Finally," he shouted. "I was beginning to wonder about you after you dissed Leigh's fine ass. Speaking of Leigh, would you mind if I tried to tap that?" he said, trying to get a reaction out of me.

"Look, man, I'm not tryin' to hit nothin'," I said, ignoring his comment about Leigh. "I'm just hangin' out. She told me she wanted to go to the beach, and I said okay," I explained.

"I don't give a damn. Don't nobody take a girl to a beach fifteen miles from where they live, this late at night, without tryin' to do something. Either you lying, or you ain't got no dick," he said, biting his tongue as Victoria walked back with his phone in hand.

"Is she alright?" Mike asked, dropping the subject.

"Yeah, she was a little worried, but she's okay now," Victoria informed him.

"Well, kids," Mike said with a yawn, "I'm glad everything is okay. I'll see you later, Vicki—I mean, Victoria. Rome, I'll holla at you later. I'm 'bout to tear dat ass up," he whispered in my ear as we gave each other the one-handed hug that "macho" guys like to use.

"I heard some of what he said. No offense, but your friend is so nasty," Victoria said as Mike walked away.

"He's not that bad. You just don't know him like I do. He's a cool dude."

"Well, I heard what he was telling you, and to me, that is so nasty. Tell me this, would you want your sister to—"

Before she could finish her thought, I blurted an emphatic, "Hell, no!"

"But that's not to say he's not a good guy. If I had a sister, I wouldn't want her dating anybody, so I'm pretty much biased in that department. Why are we talking about this, anyway? I don't wanna talk about Mike's nasty ass right now," I said as Victoria giggled.

"Yeah, me neither," she said, still chuckling.

"You about ready to go?" I asked. She nodded her head.

"So where am I taking you?" I asked as we got inside the car.

"After hearing what Mike plans on doing with Cassandra tonight, I don't wanna go home to listen to that again. What do you think we should do?"

I wanted her to just come out and ask if we could go back to my place. Even though I hadn't planned on doing anything sexual with her, I wanted *her* to ask so it wouldn't seem like I was getting any ides or just had sex on the brain like Mike.

We sat there, with the engine running, pretending as if going back to my house wasn't the only realistic idea—what with the late hour and all.

After about ten minutes of "It's too late to go to a club, we *are* kind of sandy, and it *is* kind of late," she granted my wish. "Would you mind if I crashed at your place?"

I rushed to say, "I got a couple extra rooms, so that wouldn't be a problem."

10

A Slumber Party

"How come British people have accents when they talk, but when they sing they sound American?" I heard JC saying as I approached my front door.

He was alone, talking to himself, so I motioned at Victoria, and we watched him through the screen door. I rolled my eyes at her, and she snickered.

"So, are you a beach person?" he said, again with no one in sight.

"Okay, answer me this—how come a pretty lady like you is single?" he said, and then I heard a rumble from the bathroom.

Michelle walked back into the room; JC perked up and leaned back to make himself look cooler and more carefree. She took a seat near him and he turned all his attention on her.

"How come British people sing when they have accents, but don't when they sing, but Americans don't when they do?" JC stuttered her way.

When Michelle turned a puzzled look his way, I had to contain my laughter. JC then went to his Plan B conversation starter.

"You like the beach?" he asked weakly.

Michelle gave a bland, "Yes."

"Why don't you have a man?" he asked her, reeking of desperation for a reply.

Michelle was obviously tired from a long day, JC's lack of personality, or both. As much as she looked like she was enjoying his company before, was as much as she seemed bored and unimpressed now. It was as if his "un-coolness" had finally kicked in, and she didn't want to be bothered anymore. She was about to blow him off, but before she shattered his confidence even more, I decided to step in.

"I need to help that boy out. He's dying in there," I told Victoria. She covered her mouth to keep from laughing.

"Please do," she insisted, holding back her laughter. "His game is awful."

I made a couple of sounds walking towards the door so I wouldn't startle them.

"Wassup, you guys?" I said. Michelle jumped out of her seat and greeted me as if I'd just saved her from a burning building.

"Where's Victoria?" she asked, looking around and outside, as if she wanted to talk to anybody besides JC.

"She's outside, looking at the stars," I lied.

Michelle ran out the door and down the four steps in front of the house with the speed and precision of an NFL defensive end. I envisioned her sacking Victoria like Lawrence Taylor before returning my attention to JC.

"So how's it going?" I asked softly, as though I were talking to a five-year-old.

"It's all good," he said with confidence as hollow as his tone.

I didn't know what to tell him, and besides that, how I would tell it to him? "Man, your game is terrible" wouldn't work and would have been just plain mean. That was something Mike would say.

As we tried to figure out what to say to one another, I wondered if JC and I were even friends. I had known Mike since middle school, and he always brought JC around, but at no point in time did I remember it ever being JC and I alone, without Mike. It had been Mike and I, or JC and Mike plenty of times. But had there ever been JC and Roman? Hell, I didn't even have the boy's phone number, and while I had been to his house, I'd be a dead man if my life depended on knowing its exact location.

JC and I were speechless. We were like two nervous kids waiting to see the principal. And while I'm sure he was silently going over what went wrong, I couldn't wait for reinforcements.

Victoria and Michelle were still outside, talking loud enough for us to know they were out there, but low enough not to understand what they were saying.

After what seemed an eternity, Mike made his presence known. "Where the motherfuckin' party at?" He had a bottle of liquor in each hand. Cassandra walked behind to keep him from falling—he was obviously drunk.

Mike and Cassandra's arrival gave Michelle and Victoria incentive to return. I was shocked that everybody seemed wide-eyed, given the late hour, but even more surprised that Mike and Cassandra were here, considering what Mike had told me at the beach. *He's not using any room in this house,* I thought to myself as we gathered in my living room.

Since Mike wasn't horizontal yet, I knew he'd want to "continue the party." He could drink all night if given the right circumstances, and hanging out with girls was definitely an opportunity in his eyes.

"So, what are we gonna do?" Mike said loudly enough to drown out the Maroon 5 softly playing in the background. "'Cause I'm ready to get into something." He playfully smacked Cassandra on the behind before rubbing his crotch, a move I'm sure he thought masculine, but actually reminiscent of a horny gorilla in the wild.

Cassandra must have liked it rough, because she seemed to get a little hot after Mike did it. "Let's play a game," she suggested.

"How about Monopoly?" Michelle recommended.

"There ain't no fuckin' way I'm playing Monopoly, 'less it's strip Monopoly!" Mike said, laughing and slapping JC's palm.

"Yeah, girl, he's right. I'd rather go to bed than play Monopoly. That game is too long and boring, and it's way too late," Cassandra punctuated her speech with a loud popping of her chewing gum.

"Maybe we should just go home," Michelle said, looking at her watch, "It is late, and I do have to be up early tomorrow."

"Why you trying to ruin the party?" Mike interjected. "Ain't nobody going anywhere," he said with the assurance of a bank robber. "We're gonna stay here and get our thang-thang on, and that's that! Nobody wouldn't be here if they weren't down to have a good time. Plus, I'm not sure how much longer my man Rome is gonna be in town, so let's figure this out, so everybody can be happy."

If Mike used his leadership abilities for something constructive, the boy could lead the next Million Man March, I thought to myself, trying to figure out a game that would appease everyone.

"You got liquor, right, Rome?" Mike shouted over the Jay-Z now playing.

"There's vodka in the freezer and some juice in the fridge," I responded, bobbing my head to the beat.

I didn't know where the vodka had come from. It could have been a hundred years old, but since it was liquor, and not milk, it would be okay.

"Cool! We got alcohol and women! Now all we need is a game, and we can get this party started," Mike said.

"JC, think of some shit, for a change!" he shouted at JC. JC looked scared.

"Leave him alone!" Victoria and I insisted.

"He hasn't said anything to you, Mike," I told him.

"It's not like you've had any good ideas, either," Victoria reminded him.

"You right. I haven't, but I'm going by track record, which proves if it weren't for me, JC wouldn't be shit. Not saying he is now, but without me, he wouldn't be half the shit he is today," Mike said, laughing.

"Quit it, Mike," I warned.

"Yeah, that's enough, Mike!" Cassandra added.

"I ain't lyin'. Shit, ask the nigga," Mike said, a coy expression on his face.

"You're cold, Mike. That's supposed to be your boy, and you gonna bust him out in front of everybody, again? I don't care how much alcohol you've had, you need to quit that junk, man. It's not cool," I said--and I wasn't joking.

"Aw-ight, man. I'll leave his lil ass alone," Mike said, looking at JC with a villainous smirk.

JC shook his head. It was as though Mike had a stranglehold on his manhood. They had a dysfunctional big brother/little brother dynamic. I could only imagine what it was like when I wasn't around. But then again maybe it was better. Maybe Mike was showing off for the room full of people, and me for that matter.

When it was mentioned before, I laughed it off, figuring a room full of people could come up with a better idea, but fifteen minutes later, Mike's strip poker idea turned out to be the best suggestion of the night.

Suddenly though, JC yelled "What about Truth or Dare?"

He hadn't said much all night, but to me, it was a clutch idea. Anything was better than the possibility of seeing anyone in that room—besides Victoria—naked.

"Hell, yeah! Truth or Dare!" Mike roared. "I haven't played that shit since high school. Ya'll down?" he said to the ladies, who nodded.

"What about you, Rome?" Mike asked.

"Hey, let's do it. I'm not gonna be the one that ruins the party," I informed him.

"So, how ya'll wanna do this?" Mike excitedly said, rising to his feet.

"Who's first?" said Cassandra.

Before she could finish her sentence, Mike was already volunteering. *That boy would do damn near anything for some tail*, I thought to myself.

"Okay, now somebody has to ask him a question," I said, looking at Cassandra.

Getting the clue, Cassandra said, "Yeah, I'll ask the first question. But where I come from, we play Truth or Dare a little differently."

"Girl, you from LA—talkin' bout where I'm from," Mike said with a few chuckles.

"Anyways," she said, glaring at Mike, "where I'm from, we play Truth or Dare a little bit different. You can ask multiple people multiple questions or dares. If you ask four people a dare at once, then those four people have to do their dares, and then all four people get to dare you to do something. You get it?" she asked us, giving the room a once over to make sure her directions were understood.

"Aight, I'm wit that," Mike said. The rest of us nodded.

I didn't know if everyone in the room was as skeptical as I was, but having been around Cassandra a couple times, I knew her version of the game wouldn't be the semi-innocent one I played as a teenager. I mean, come on. She was messing around with Mike, and I wasn't sure which of them was the bigger freak.

"Look," I told Cassandra, "there's no way in hell I'm kissing, touching, or rubbing anyone of these guys, anywhere—period!" I pointed towards Mike and JC. "Nothing's getting close to my butt, I'm not doing anything with animals, and I am not taking anything off," I continued, as the girls giggled in amusement.

"I wouldn't do that to you," Cassandra chuckled. But I wasn't fully convinced.

"Let's just get started." Michelle said, sounding as if she just wanted to get the whole thing over with.

"Mike? You said you were gonna start. Are you ready?" Cassandra said. Mike stood and readied himself for the looming question.

"Truth or dare?" she quizzed Mike.

"Dare," Mike shouted back, as though he were talking to a drill sergeant.

"I want you to drink the rest of this vodka," she said, handing him the bottle he had been sipping on since he had gotten there.

Without hesitation, he unscrewed the lid and began gulping, which had more than enough alcohol left in it to make everyone in the room a cocktail or two. We cringed as the clear liquid left the bottle and entered his system

"He's staying at your house, right?" I asked Cassandra, envisioning the sickness that was going to ensue.

She hadn't answered by the time the last drop of alcohol passed Mike's palate. Afterwards, he looked at all of us for his turn at questioning or daring, not yet showing any ill effects from the vodka.

He turned to me. "Ro-man?" His voice broke as the liquor made its way into his blood stream. "Truth or dare?" he mumbled.

"Truth," I responded. There was no way in hell it was going to be a dare.

"Aw, you're a bitch," he slurred. "Okay, then, nigga; tell me this. Who would you rather be with? Victoria or Leigh?"

Shocked he would put my business out there like that, I simply sat there. Drunk or not, he had gone too far. Determined not to let my disgust show, I answered without a hint of anger.

"Well, being that one is like a sister to me, and the other isn't, I'm gonna have to go with Victoria," I said smoothly.

Mike was annoyed that he hadn't flustered me. He rolled his eyes and took a seat.

"My turn?" I said, scanning the room for potentials.

It being my turn, having a vengeful mind, and knowing Mike as well as I did, I decided revenge would be sweet. I knew what I was going to do, but it would have to fall into place perfectly.

"Truth or dare?" I asked JC with crossed fingers, hoping he would choose right.

"Uh, dare, I guess," he said, following Mike's lead, as I had hoped he would.

"I want you to drop your pants and show Michelle and Cassandra what you're working with," I said.

All three ladies began giggling as they digested my shocking request. I knew JC was going to be apprehensive about it, which became more evident as his face reddened in embarrassment.

"Nobody wants to see his lil' dick," Mike shouted, coming to his feet. "If ya'll wanna see some real beef, ask me to do the same thing," he boasted, holding his crotch. To his chagrin, all of the ladies' attention was focused on JC. I knew they weren't the least bit attracted to JC, but that didn't keep them from being fascinated by whether he would or wouldn't complete the dare.

They paid Mike little attention. The anticipation of would he or wouldn't he swelled. Again, Mike yelled, "I'll drop 'trou'. All right, one of ya'll ask me to drop 'trou' right now, and I will. Shit, I don't know why ya'll wanna see him when I got a beef stick tucked away in my pants."

He was like a child begging for attention.

"JC, when they done with your small ass, tell them to come see my behemoth," Mike said, and laughed hysterically. No one else joined in.

Spurred on by Mike's words, JC unzipped his pants and faced Cassandra and Michelle. Victoria covered her face while Michelle and Cassandra stared at his crotch.

"Oh, my," Cassandra said. Michelle sat back, stunned.

"Vee, look!" Michelle grabbed Victoria's arms so she could see.

After a couple seconds of trying her best to avoid the view, she finally succumbed to temptation and peaked through her fingers.

"Wow," she said. Part of me hoped she thought it was small, but I knew better.

"Fuck this," Mike said, rushing to where JC was giving his presentation. He grinned and unbuttoned his pants. "I'm gonna show them something really good," he said, to no one in particular.

Two seconds later, Mike was standing next to JC, his pants down, showing himself to the ladies. As Mike arched his back like a proud Greek god, the ladies looked surprised—and amused.

"Oh, my God. Look at this!" Michelle said to Victoria, who had covered her face again. "Is that all?" Michelle asked Cassandra, and chuckled. "That's what's been making you do all that moaning? Girl, you deserve an Academy Award, 'cause I don't care how much motion in the ocean there is, that little boat would never make it off the dock for me," Michelle said, barely containing her laughter.

"Girl, shut up! He's gonna hear you!" Cassandra warned Michelle. Cassandra was the only one of us, besides the two flashers, who wasn't either laughing or trying not to, but that changed when Michelle kept jabbing her with her pinky, impersonating Mike's manhood.

JC and Mike, by now, had covered themselves and were wondering what was going on.

Right on cue, Mike again opened his big mouth, confident that he was the reason the ladies were in a giggling huddle.

"See how I got them chickens clucking?" Mike said arrogantly to JC. "Never bring a knife to a gun fight, boy."

"Whatever!" was JC's only come back. He must have been a stern believer in the unwritten man's rule of "no looking down." Hell, I was too, but I had seen the expressions on the girls faces and knew better.

I remembered the day, years ago, that I first realized Mike probably came up a short in the manhood department. We'd been hanging out at his house, and I'd stumbled across several bottles of penile enlargement capsules in his messy room. It wasn't until now that my brain had a reason to recall that day. But, I had no idea about JC--I just took a blind shot in the dark.

“What’s next on the docket? Anybody else want a private show by the ding-a-ling king?” Mike winked.

“Actually, we’re all kinda tired. We were hoping we could take a rain check on the rest of the game,” Michelle announced.

“Rain check?” Mike shouted. “Nah. Fuck that! I was hoping whoever had the biggest titties could take the dude with the biggest dick, and they could do a lil’ sumthin-sumthin. You know—kinda like the prom king and queen.”

We all knew he was drunk and being more offensive than usual because of it, but that comment even had me shaking my head, wondering what he was thinking.

All three girls had steam rising from the tops of their heads. They had been biting their tongues all the night at Mike’s asinine comments and distasteful behavior. He was in for it, and he had brought it on himself.

“No, this little-dicked mutha-fucka did not just say that!” Michelle roared. “If you think that Vienna sausage in your pants is anything but small, you got more problems that I ever imagined.”

“And the bad thing is, it’s small and ugly,” Cassandra said. The girls erupted into laughter. “King ding-a-ling? That thing looks like a little beef jerky,” she said, looking towards Mike’s crotch and laughing even harder.

“What was I thinking? Look, Mike, it’s really not gonna work between us; I need someone a little more—grown up,” Cassandra finished, and they all giggled again.

JC, Victoria, Mike, and I were silent as Michelle and Cassandra continued their verbal assault. They were giving him a taste of his own medicine, and he had to stand there and take it. A man's manhood was a sensitive subject.

“I’m ready to go. What about you guys?” Cassandra asked Michelle and Victoria, who agreed.

“Umm, JC? Michelle and I were wondering if you wanted to come back to our place and hang out for a while,” Cassandra said as they again giggled.

Startled, but still a man, JC agreed, and was, I'm sure, thinking with the head that got him into that position in the first place.

As they exited, Victoria pulled me to her. "I'm going to go to the bathroom," she whispered.

"First door on the left," I told her as she grinned and walked into the hall.

Mike was the only one left without a place to go, although he could have always just gone home.

"Mike, what are you gonna do?" I asked. "You can always stay here if you need to."

"I'm cool," he said, bewildered. "I can't believe that mutha-fucka. I taught that boy well," he said to himself, convinced his tutelage was the reason for JC's conquest. Then he stood up. "Look, man, I'm cool. I'm going to hit the road. Don't worry. I'm not drunk any more."

I didn't know whether to believe him or not. The shock of "the student" defeating "the master" could have knocked the alcohol out of his system. Then again, he might have been as drunk now as before. I didn't know what to do. He wasn't noticeably wobbling or anything, and his speech was leaps and bounds better than fifteen minutes before the game. But on the other hand I really didn't want him there, not after what had just went down. Without much debate from him or myself, he decided he was going to leave, and I didn't try to stop him.

Mike walked out the front door, still believing he was behind JC's success, and I immediately shifted my attention back to Victoria. With what had just transpired, I wondered if she still wanted to stay the night, but I found her preparing for bed in the back room.

"I see you found the guestroom," I said to Victoria.

I was as nervous as a hooker in church, but played it as cool as I could. I didn't know what I expected to happen, and it had been a while since I'd felt this awkward with a woman--what with the late hour. I was nervous, cautious, and curious--at the same time.

"You already know the bathroom's down the hall, and my room is right across from it, so if you need anything just yell or knock on my door," I briefed her.

"Okay, I will," she said with a smile. "Thanks again for letting me stay here. God only knows what they're doing over there with JC."

"No problem. There are shorts and shirts in the drawer if you don't wanna sleep in your clothes," I told her. "Matter of fact, let me grab a pair of those shorts, too." I smiled. "I usually sleep--you know...But since I have company, I'll wear these so you don't get the wrong idea."

"You don't have to rearrange your life for me, Roman, and if I decide to come to your room, I'll be sure to knock."

"Okay," I smiled, a little embarrassed. "Have a good night, and I'll see you in the morning."

"Okay, and thanks again," she said. I turned off the light and walked out.

Just as my head hit the pillow, I heard Victoria shout my name from the other room.

"Roman, are you still awake?" Her voice fluttered through the hollow night.

"What's up?" I said, walking into her room, using the hall light for illumination.

"Sorry to bother you, but I was wondering if I could have a glass of water. I tried to get up, but I couldn't see the light switches, and I didn't want to stub my toe or something walking in the dark," she said sheepishly.

"Yeah, of course." I walked out and returned with a glass of water. "Is there anything else I can get for you?" I asked as she drank the water and lay back down.

"No, but thanks," she said, pulling the covers back over her.

"Well, good night again." I closed the door and walked back to my room. Minutes later, I heard my name echoing through the walls again.

"What can I do for you?" I asked Victoria, noticing her leg poking from underneath the covers as she lay there wearing a pair of my old high school gym shorts.

"I hate to bother you, again, but I was wondering if you were going to take me home in the morning, or if I needed to call someone for a ride."

"Come on now. What kind of guy would I be if I didn't take you home in the morning? I'm insulted by the mere thought," I jokingly said. "Don't worry. I'll take you home whenever you want."

"Okay, thanks, Roman." She got up, exposing her small but shapely body, which was draped in a t-shirt I hadn't been able to fit since junior high.

"You're welcome," I said. Blood rushed from my brain and feet, causing me to immediately evacuate the room. I used the old "put it in the waist line of my pants" trick as I scurried back to my room, trying to avoid embarrassment.

I lay motionless for the next couple of minutes, waiting for Victoria's next request, and I began thinking about Leigh. It seemed like forever since our last conversation, and to be quite honest, I missed her. I understood what she meant when she said, "we haven't talked in a while" after only a day.

I also began thinking about when I would leave. I had come for an emergency with no real timetable for departure, and I had been gone long enough to make "getting back home" more of a realistic decision than when I first arrived.

A soft knock rattled my door enough for me to lose focus.

"Roman, are you asleep?" Victoria whispered as she inched into my room, careful not to stub her toe.

"No," I replied in a groggy voice. "What can I do for you?" I could see her faint silhouette in the night.

"I forgot to give you something," she said, making her way to my bed.

"What is it?" I asked, anticipating.

"Hold out your hands and close your eyes," she whispered. Anxiety flooded my body.

"What is it?" I asked again, shutting my eyes and baring my palms.

“This.” She leaned over and gently kissed my lips.

There was no preparing myself for her advance. Was it really happening, or would the lights suddenly click on and the room flood with a camera crew and laughing participants?

“Can I open my eyes yet?” I asked, my mouth quivering for another kiss, palms leaking sweat.

“No, not yet,” she said, taking my hands and placing them on her breasts. “Now you can open them,” she whispered. I began to caress her bare chest.

When I opened my eyes, she was sitting on my bed—totally naked.

I wondered how she got undressed so quickly without me knowing. “Do you like touching me?” she asked, then gave a joyous gasp at the sensual touches I was giving her.

“Uh-huh,” I returned. My shorts got tighter and tighter, reminding me why shorts worn in high school were bad for a young man going through puberty.

She reached into my pants, began petting, and lay down next to me. We were touching, rubbing, and prodding - discovering new things about each other’s bodies.

Her moans increased as my middle and ring fingers tantalized her. I was ready for the foreplay to end, but she reached into my pants and began stroking me.

Victoria knew what she was doing. The problem was that I didn’t know what I was doing. I wasn’t a virgin, but I was inexperienced. I was hot, and I was ready to -"Uhh"- come!

I sat up and pulled back, forcing her hand to vacate my pants. “I—uh—need to go see something,” I said, rushing out of the room, trying to keep from revealing the problem. Since she was in the room where my clothes were, I had to wear a pair of underwear I hadn’t worn in years—a pair of “duh-dun-ta-duns,” as we called them as kids because of their resemblance to Superman’s red drawers.

I changed underwear as fast as I could and hurried back to my room.

“Everything okay?” Victoria asked, puzzled.

"Yeah, everything's cool, but there's one problem—I don't have any condoms."

"You don't?" she returned, disappointed. "Not even one?"

"I wish. I searched the whole house, and nothing. I don't live here, remember?" I reminded her, adding a little more legitimacy to the story.

And while I hadn't searched at all for condoms, I was sure I wouldn't have found any if I had. Which was okay, considering what I had just done in my pants.

"That's too bad," Victoria said as I lay back down next to her. "It could have been interesting."

After putting her borrowed clothes back on, Victoria and I talked about ourselves a little more before she finally fell asleep. I stayed up a little longer, watching her dream and wondering what could have been.

I thought about a lot of things that night, as I lay wrapped in the sheets and blankets with Victoria. I had been doing so many things I wasn't used to doing that I had almost forgotten I had another life in Texas, and other friends I wanted to see here in San Diego. If it wasn't Leigh, it was Mike, Victoria, or my parents—it was always something. But I was going to have to go sometime soon, whether I liked it or not. The longer I waited the more withdrawal I was going to have.

"I hope you don't think I do that with just anybody, Roman," Victoria told me as I got into my car to take her home. "'Cause I don't. Believe me," she told me, her stern eyes revealing her sincerity.

"Don't worry. I don't have one negative thought about you."

I didn't know how to tell her I was leaving. Hell, I didn't know until early that morning. She looked so peaceful staring out the window. We drove through neighborhood after neighborhood of trees and breathtaking greenery.

"I had forgotten San Diego was this beautiful during the day," I said, breaking a few moments of pleasant silence.

"The first time I came to your house, it was dark so I didn't notice all these trees."

"It's nice, isn't it," she said, entranced by the landscape, as though I had stolen the thought right out of her head.

"Yep, it really is." I was stalling. I didn't want to tell her my departure plans.

I kept going over the best way to tell Victoria I was leaving. I had known her less than a week, and in the imaginary conversations I had had with her, I hadn't had this problem. Who was I kidding? She may have not been my girlfriend, but at the very least, she was a good friend. I was more lost now than when I was wasting away in Texas just days ago.

Victoria, Leigh, my parents, my brother/nephew. Should I stay, or should I go? At this point, Uncle Sin and his strip club fetish seemed like fun. At least I knew what to expect from a night with him, minus the occasional trans-gender mishap.

"Roman," Victoria said, just as I uttered her name. We chuckled lightly, then began the expected patter—"no, you first," "no, no, you go ahead."

"Okay," she said, finally agreeing to speak first. "I really like you, Roman, and I was wondering, you know—how you felt about this, or us, or whatever." Her cheeks reddened like the face of a Raggedy Ann doll. "I would like to spend more time with you and see if you're the real deal. I don't know—never mind." She turned away, as if fear had gotten the best of her. Two seconds later, she turned back around. "I don't wanna scare you or anything," she said. "I'm just curious to know what you're thinking."

The only response I had was to ask directions to her apartment. I had never been happier not knowing where someone lived. If not for that, our ride would have been more uncomfortable than it already was, and I would have had to answer her questions.

As I pulled up to her complex, I still hadn't answered. The awkward silence finally became too much.

"Umm—" I mumbled as she waited for an answer.

"Umm?" she mocked. "Forget it. I knew I shouldn't have said anything," she told me, sounding more hurt than angry. "Have a good day." She opened the car door.

"Wait!" I pleaded, softly grabbing her wrist and ushering her back into the car. "Victoria, I'm leaving tomorrow. I made my reservation this morning while you were asleep. That was what I wanted to tell you before. But after you told me what you did, I didn't know how to tell you."

"Oh, well, don't worry about it," Victoria said. "If you've got to leave, then that's what you have to do."

"Wait a second. I'm not finished yet," I told her. "I wanted to tell you how good it's been hanging out with you. You know what my life's been like back in Houston. The time we've spent together has been great for me—damn near therapeutic. I can honestly say that meeting you has been one of the highlights of this trip." She glanced at me, and I continued.

"But I have to go. I have to get back home to *my* life. It's been good being here all these days, but this isn't home for me anymore. The sooner I get back, the easier the transition will be. I don't want this to sound like goodbye. If anything, it's the start of something new and exciting."

"New? How is this?" Victoria said abruptly. "Never mind. Just go back to Texas, to your uncle, to your great job. Just go, Roman. Go and do what's best for you!"

"Victoria, hold on," I begged. "Victoria! Victoria, hold on for a second." She stormed toward her house.

Before I could unbuckle my seatbelt and put the car in park, she was inside. I decided not to run after her; I had nothing special to say to her except "sorry." I had done more apologizing in the last week than in the previous twenty-five years of my life, and my father wanted to "give me a surprise." Shit. Instead of chasing after Victoria, I went to meet my father, again, just to get it over with.

11

Meeting Mathew

"Good morning!" my father's chipper voice boomed.

"Hey, Dad," I said lethargically. He had come outside to greet me as I approached.

"How's it going, son? I hope you're not too tired from last night," he said, as if he had a surveillance team following me.

"What do you mean by that?" I snapped at him, wondering what, if anything, he knew about last night.

"Don't worry, son. I'm glad you and your friends had fun. You deserve a bit of fun. Hell, when I was your age—" Before he could finish, I cut him off.

"Dad, did you have somebody come by and check up on me? That's just like you to do some sneaky shit like that," I yelled. It was the second time I'd directed profanity towards my father in as many days. My emotions ran wild when I talked to him. I just couldn't help it.

"Hold on a minute!" he roared. "I'm still your father, and you will—"

"Respect me as such, I know, I know," I said, finishing his sentence, adding water to a grease fire.

I didn't know why I was giving him a hard time; I couldn't care less if he knew what I was doing. I guess it was too early, and I was stressed over things with Victoria and Leigh.

He held his tongue and calmly said, "Nosey Mrs. Stephens from across the street called last night. I told her I knew what was going on and that I was sorry if things were too noisy."

I was shocked at his patience. He was really trying to repair our broken relationship.

"Don't worry. Things didn't get too out of control or anything. I just had a few friends over. We sat around drinking and listening to music."

"You don't have to tell me, son. I know you're a responsible young man. I had no doubt that you would have things under control," he told me.

"So what's the big surprise?"

"I think it just woke up," he said as he turned and headed inside. "Mathew, this is your big brother, Roman." He picked the little boy up and checked his bottom for wetness. "Say hi, Mathew," my father coached. Mathew stared at me with glazed, freshly awakened eyes. He was exact color of creamed coffee.

"This is the surprise, son." He smiled at me. "I wanted you to meet your brother. He reminds me so much of you at this age. Doesn't cry much at all, huh, Mathew?" he said, pitching his voice low. "You want to hold him? He doesn't bite, unless you have canned peaches in front of him," he said, trying to be funny.

"No, I'm okay. I don't wanna drop him or anything," I said.

"Drop him? He's your baby brother, not a football!" he said, shoving him into my arms, forcing me to hold him. "See, it's not so bad is it? My boys, finally together," he said, looking like a proud papa. "And it only took two years," he chuckled.

With that comment, I gave him back his son and walked into the den to escape what felt like immense pressure.

That son of a bitch. God, he pisses me off. What does he expect from me? I sat down and turned on the television.

Soon after, my father walked in, still holding Mathew, who was still trying to wake up. As I watched a man try to sell a bald spot remover and a food dehydrator to his amazed audience, my father began to ramble.

"Any games on today? It's been so long since I've had the chance to watch any sports. I'm so busy with your brother, work, and church that I don't even have time to play racquetball anymore, which is why I've put on a couple pounds since you last saw me." He patted his newfound gut. "What season is it, anyways? Are there any games on?" he asked, sounding sports illiterate.

"It's baseball season right now, but there aren't any games on." I informed him as I flipped through the channels, and put down the remote, giving up hope for any Saturday sports entertainment.

The three of us stared at the lifeless screen. I figured that learning about my little brother, or cousin, or whatever the politically correct term for him was, was better than wasting away in front of a blank screen. I knew the way I was acting towards him wasn't right. Cause the reality was we were both victims in this whole mess.

"So why have you been watching him so much? Where is his mother? I mean, Aunt Emily," I asked.

"She started a new job not too long ago, and she's been putting in a lot of hours. Since I didn't want my son going to some filthy nursery, I've been working less and taking more responsibility for your brother," he told me.

I was uncomfortable every time he referred to him as my brother, almost as if he were forcing it. There could be a river of my blood flowing through his veins, but I didn't know him at all.

"Well, that's good, Dad. I'm glad you're taking such an active roll in your son's life," I told him, sounding more like Oprah than Roman Sullivan. In spite of myself, the kid had kind of softened me up.

"Did you say you're going to church now?" I asked, putting the finishing touch on my Oprah-inspired speech.

"Yeah, church has been good for me; it's allowed me to ask for forgiveness and admit my wrong-doings. You should come to my church sometime. I think it might do you some good, too," he said, sounding like I were the one with the illegitimate son with the sister of my ex-wife.

"Yeah, maybe," I said, to appease and shut him up. "But it's going to have to be next time I visit, because I'm going home tomorrow. I already booked my flight."

"When were you planning to tell me? After you left?" he asked, straightening, as if to say, "this is serious."

"No, I was going to tell you before I left. That's why I'm telling you now," I said. "You didn't think I was going to stay forever, did you?"

"Well, not forever," he said, loosening his stance. "I was just hoping we could do more catching up, ya know? Try and make up for some of the time we've lost."

"Well, like I said, it's going to have to wait until next time."

"Next time, huh? So what you're telling me is the next time I see you, your brother will be—what? Five? Six?"

I hated the way he was using Mathew as leverage. If he wanted me to stay longer, he should just say it, instead of using an innocent child.

"Let's be real with each other. Do you think you can do that for me?" he asked.

"I'm not the one who's been lying, Dad. You don't have to worry about me telling the truth," I said bluntly. "That's never been hard for me."

"You're right; it has never been a problem for you. I'll give you that. But you still haven't answered my question. When are you coming back? Can you answer that without bringing up something else I've done wrong?

"I can't answer right now 'cause I just don't know," I told him.

"You don't know?" he said with frustration. "That's too bad, son. A lot of people would love to see you come home from time to time—especially your mother."

"Don't even, Dad," I fired at him, trying to control my voice. I didn't want to startle Mathew.

"Don't even what?"

"Don't try to use her as a tool to keep me here—her, or Mathew—not when you're the reason things are the way they are. Look, I gotta go. Give your son a kiss for me." With that, I walked out of his house and to my car.

"At least you said good-bye this time," he yelled, covering Mathew's ears.

Without even a glance in his direction, I began to pull away. Over the roar of the engine, I dimly heard my father yell, "Go ahead! Run away again, like a coward!"

Coward echoed in my mind, bouncing against every part of my being, ending at my heart. "Coward?" I said, throwing the car into a hard park. "You have the audacity to call me a coward?" I yelled, charging towards his door.

He ushered Mathew into the house as if we were about to have a gunfight. After closing the door, he turned and looked at me.

"Dad, please tell me you didn't just call me a coward--*especially* in front of Mathew," I said. "Please, Dad—tell me that."

Something about the word *coward* got my blood boiling—as I thought it should any man. It was as disrespectful as calling a woman a bitch.

He was silent and motionless. Then he confessed. "Yeah, I did, son."

"How in the fuck can you call me, or anybody, a coward?" I yelled.

"Because cowards run in the face of adversity, son," he said monotonously. "And no matter what you think about me, your mother, your brother—whoever—you ran when it got a little rough. I call a spade, a spade," he said smugly.

"A little rough? If this is 'a little rough,' I'd hate to see what constitutes something big. And I didn't run. I just couldn't be here any more, not with how things were going. I mean, Mom ain't "Mom" no more, and you ain't the dad I grew up with. What did you expect me to do, go to family counseling?"

"I'm not your dad anymore?" he said—as if that were the only thing he heard in my speech. "I'm more of a dad then you will ever know!"

He continued. "You think I've been such a bad father, huh? Well, you're the one who don't know anything. I tried to keep this family together!" he roared as a tear rolled down his cheek. "I tried my best!" With that, he turned and walked back into the house.

I wanted to go after him and finish our verbal joust, but I had never seen my father get that worked up before, not even when I lost his Hank Aaron and Reggie Jackson rookie cards as a kid. I went back to my still-running vehicle, wondering what my father meant. He tried to keep the family together?

I decided to play detective and see what my aunt Emily had to say. Although her actions disgusted me, I figured a hot shower after talking to her would help wash away the filth of close contact with her. Even if she had nothing to say, it was a shot worth taking.

"Hey, Romy," my aunt Emily said, opening the door. "It's good to see you." She smiled and extended her arms for a hug.

Hugging her felt weird. Although I felt as though I should hate her, she had been my favorite aunt before all the drama. As a kid, I used to wish I had a twin, just so I could be like her and my mom. Someone to play with, someone to take tests for me in school, someone to double date with—all the cool things twins did on television and in movies. While she and my mother were close and shared a lot of things, I don't think my father was something my aunt should have helped herself to.

"How long have you been in town?" she asked me.

"About five or six days. I'm actually leaving tomorrow."

"So soon, huh? I wish you'd have come by earlier, but I'm just happy to see your face after all these years. How have you been? How is Texas treating you?"

"It's treating me okay, I guess. I just had to get used to the summers and all the rain, ya know."

"Mmm-hmm, I heard that. You never really miss Southern California until you have to deal with the weather somewhere else," she said, fanning herself as though she could feel the Texas heat.

"But anyways, I came by to ask you a question," I said.

"Yeah, baby? What it is?" she asked.

"I was over at my dad's house this morning, and he said something that was pretty out of the blue. I wanted to see if you knew anything about it."

"Oh, you went over there?" she said gleefully. "So you finally got to meet your little brother?" She was doing it now, too. I wanted to roll my eyes, but reframed.

"Uh, yeah, I did, but that wasn't my question. While I was there, my father and I exchanged words, and he said he tried his best to keep the family together. I thought that was weird, considering what went on between you guys. Do you have any idea what he meant?"

Without even thinking about it, she said, "Sorry, but I don't know what he was talking about." She shifted in her chair. "But while we're on the subject, I've wanted to apologize to you for years. I just never felt the time was right. I just want you to know I never meant to hurt you, or anybody else. I made a mistake and I'm gonna have to deal with it for the rest of my life."

Don't worry about it, Auntie. I never blamed you, at least not completely, I thought. Aloud, I said, "My father is the one who needs to apologize. Anyway, I gotta get going. I have a few loose ends I need to tie up before I leave tomorrow."

"Okay. Sorry I couldn't help you. Your father and I only communicate when necessary—when Mathew needs to be picked up or odds and ends here and there. But have a good trip; I hope I see you again and hopefully it'll be sooner than three years, okay?"

"Okay," I agreed, hugging her before I left.

As I stepped out of my car, I heard "Seven! Come on, seven!"

"Nah, you mean snake eyes!"

"Uhn, that's what I'm talkin' bout. Gimme my money!"

Mike, Earl, and Mo were kneeling down, playing craps as though my house were a back alley. Before I could ask why the hell they were bringing down the property value of my home by shooting craps in broad daylight, Mike jumped to his feet and began explaining.

"Man, where were you?" he said. "I called you four times. I wanted to see if you were gonna be available to go somewhere with me."

I wasn't in the mood for more surprises. However, I didn't want to be bothered with Mo and Earl either, so I just went along.

"And who's driving to this surprise?" I asked.

"I am," he said proudly. "Just get in, and I'll take you to it."

"All right, I'll go, but this can't take all day," I muttered.

"Where ya'll headed?" Mo asked.

"Man, it's a surprise for Rome. Not you!" Mike exclaimed.

"Oh, yeah?" Mo said, his face full of interest.

"What kinda surprise?" Earl asked, as if he were somehow going to get answers that Mo couldn't.

"One for my boy Rome," he informed them with a serious look on his face.

I hopped into Mike's car, happy that he had dealt with Mo and Earl. I was interested in what Mike could have in store for me after over ten years of no gifts at all.

I had to move a couple of things out of the passenger seat before I could sit—mainly a Big Brothers of America application and *Girls Gone Wild: Safari Edition,* DVD.

"So, where are you taking me?" I asked Mike. "'Cause if you're going to some strip club porno show, you can turn this car around right now. I'm dead serious. And I damn sure ain't goin' with you to meet any more women," I finished.

"Oh, so that's all I am to you? Porn and strippers?" he asked, as if I had offended him. "Horny-ass Mike, right? Well, I ain't gonna lie. That's a part of me. Shit, ain't nothing wrong with liking naked-ass women, but trust me—that's not all I'm about. I got dreams like everybody else. It's just nobody ever asks about them. I ain't tryin' to get all emotional and shit on your last day." His eyes looked wet, but it could have just been the reflection of the sun or that he'd just smoked. "I just wanted to give my best friend a going away gift." He smiled. "You know—something to make you wanna come back this time."

I wondered how he knew I was leaving then remembered Victoria and Cassandra were roommates. "My bad. Mike, man, you know the way you come off sometimes. I was just making sure. I wasn't trying to offend you, 'cause like you said, it is my last day."

"Don't worry about it, Rome. Just come hang with me for a while, and we'll call it even," he said.

"*Ms. Lee's Massage and Spa*," the sign read as we drove up to an older building in a questionable part of town.

"What are we doing here?" I inquired as we entered the building.

"Chill out," Mike ordered as he asked the lady at the counter for two number threes off the menu chart. "That will be one hundwed-thiwty-two dolla'," said the woman in a thick Asian accent.

I didn't know what shocked me more—Mike at a massage parlor, or Mike paying a hundred and thirty-two bucks for a massage that didn't guarantee a happy ending—or did it?

"Wight back he-ah," the lady said, steering us behind a curtain to a room with three red massage tables.

"Man, you're gonna love this!" Mike sounded giddy as he disrobed. "I like to come here whenever I get some extra cash."

"And how long have you been coming here?" I asked, anxious to know more about my friend. I thought I knew him pretty well, but us sitting in a massage parlor proved not at well as I thought.

"A couple years," he said, climbing onto one of the beds. "I was walking by one day and thought one of the chicks working here was cute. I came in to see what was up with her, and she talked me into getting a massage. It felt so good I kept coming back, even though Asian baby wasn't giving me no game. But on the real, they feel so damn good I walked out of here and felt like I got rid of all my problems."

As our masseurs walked in, Mike assured me it was going to be great before dipping his face in the table hole. I followed his lead and disrobed, eager to see if Mike was being truthful about the therapeutic capabilities of a massage.

We moaned as the stress and tension was rubbed, patted, and knuckled away. Mike wasn't lying. This was my first professional massage, and I vowed it wouldn't be my last. *If I'd had one of these a few years back, I might have never moved away,* I thought to myself as the masseur rubbed the area between my shoulder blades with her elbow.

As the massage moved towards the small of my back, I couldn't help but cry out. This lady was single-handedly rubbing away three years of frustration and anger, and she couldn't have weighed more than a hundred pounds. "Oh, my goodness!" I yelled.

"I know what you mean," Mike said. "I did the same thing the first time I came here. So wassup up with Leigh?" he asked, out of the blue.

"Why are you asking me about her now?"

"I don't know. I haven't heard you mention her in a while, and I was wondering why."

"She's cool, I guess," I said as clearly as I could through the circular tubing of the table. "To tell you the truth, we're not really on good terms right now."

"Damn, man, you went from having two women to none in less than a week," Mike said, chuckling.

"How's JC?" I asked, as payback for bringing up my woman troubles.

"He's cool, but ever since last night, he's been talkin' about his pimp aspirations—like, he seriously wants to be a 'John,'" he said. "That fool really thinks he's a player!"

"That's cool. At least he can't be your whipping boy, anymore." That much was true, even if being a player was a bit of a stretch. Still, it was kinda admirable. Getting out of Mike's grasp was a good thing.

"I guess it is time the poor bastard grew up, but I am going to miss having an assistant," Mike replied.

"And a chauffeur, and a maid, and a yes-man," I added, and we both chuckled.

"So you're really headed back to Texas, huh?" Mike asked. The hole in the table restricted my nodding, so I told him my flight left at eleven the next morning.

"And there's nothing I can do to make you stay?" he asked.

"Not unless you know a couple who wants to adopt a twenty-five-year-old man."

"Man, you know you can always stay with me and Mom," Mike generously offered.

"I appreciate the offer, but you know I can't do that," I said.

"I know; just thought I'd put it out there. So what is going on with you and your parents? I wanted to bring it up earlier this week, but I didn't know how to," he said.

"Same old. Pops is still a punk. The fool tried to say, after everything's he's done to my mom and me, that he's tried to keep us together. Can you believe that shit?"

"What about Moms? How is she doing?" he asked.

"She's the same too—still actin' weird. So I guess nothing's really changed," I said with a sigh.

"What about Houston?" he asked.

"What about it?"

"What's so good about it?"

"Nothing. And I'm serious about that. It's just not here."

I didn't want to tell him about everything that had been going on with me. And as much as I liked the one-on-one with Mike, I wasn't ready to go into full disclosure with anyone about my family. Victoria knew the most, and that was only because she had exposed her naked body to me before-hand, and Mike also knew a little, but neither knew the whole story Not that I was embarrassed about it, I just liked to follow an unwritten rule—You don't talk about things in public; you discuss them internally until there's a resolution.

"Well, we're gonna miss you out here. It ain't been the same since you left. There's no general to keep us in line," Mike said, halfway chuckling. "What are you going to do with the rest of your day? 'Cause I can plan a quick party if you want."

"Maybe next time; I promised my mom and Leigh I wouldn't leave without saying goodbye."

"Damn, I gotta go see Cassandra, too," he said.

My thumping heart made the last few minutes of my massage less enjoyable. "I have way too many people to see before I leave tomorrow," I told Mike, hoping all would go smoothly.

"I know; sounds like you might have to take a later flight," Mike said with a slight sneer.

After the ladies were done with our massages, I got up and dressed; Mike lay there, basking in the great rub down. I had just had months of tension rubbed out of my bones and muscles, but I felt the anxiety and fear seeping back in.

I rushed Mike to get up, and we were off. As soon as Mike turned the corner to my house, my foot was halfway out the door.

I thanked him and leaned over to hug him, not knowing if I would see him before I left, then I jogged to my car.

"You're welcome, man, and don't be a stranger," Mike yelled as he drove away, disappearing around the corner.

12

Keeping Secrets

Leigh, Michelle, or Mom? Who should I visit first? I thought as I turned onto the freeway, which could have taken me to see all three in about the same amount of time. Leigh was mad. So was Victoria. Instead of just admitting that I was apprehensive about confrontations with the two younger ladies, I rationalized that since my mom gave birth to me, I should see her first.

I pulled up to my mother's house and, amazingly, saw my dad's car parked in the driveway next to hers. Three years ago, that would have been normal, but to my knowledge they hadn't had a lot of contact since the divorce.

When I turned off the engine, I heard yelling and arguing inside. I eased up the walkway, hoping the muffled yelling would mutate into coherent words. Passing the window, I wondered why Aunt Emily was there. She and my mother sat next to each other as my father stood and shouted.

"I'm so sick of this crap! I'm tired of being hated by my own son for something that's not all my fault," he barked.

"It's been three years, Tony," Aunt Emily said.

"Yeah, it has been," my father interjected. "Three years since my son has seen me as his father. You two are responsible for this, just as much as me," he screamed. My mother was sniffling. Aunt Emily rolled her eyes.

"What do you want to happen after all this time?" Aunt Emily shot his way. "You want to tell everybody the truth?"

"I don't care about everybody. I care about my son! I want my son back! I've wanted him back ever since he left."

"No, Tony, please!" My mother sobbed. "You promised you wouldn't tell Roman."

"So what am I supposed to do?" My father's arms flew to the sky as if he was a referee signaling a field goal. "You convinced me that if I went along with your cockamamie story, my son would forgive me. After three years he's back, he hasn't forgiven me, and now he's leaving again for God knows how long. What should I do? I want two sons. Is that too much to ask?"

"Shit, just tell him them, Tony! I'm sick of hearing about this every time I see your ass. Roman is old enough to understand. He ain't no little boy, anymore," Aunt Emily snarled.

"No, Emily, there's got to be another way," my mother pleaded. "Roman would be so angry with me."

"Better me than you, huh, Miriam?" my father challenged. "As long as he doesn't hate you, right? Well, I'm sick of it, and I'm sick of our son hating me!"

My first thought was of betrayal. Whatever was going on involved me...And no one had the decency to inform me.

I stepped out of hiding, opened the door, and demanded the truth.

"Who's going to start first?" I yelled. They stared at me in disbelief.

"How long have you been here?" my mother asked, tears running down her face.

"Long enough. So ya'll might as well just tell me," I said.

Except for my mother's weeping, the room was silent. No one wanted to let me in on this big secret--a secret big enough to bring them all together for a discussion, like the board game *Clue*. They were really starting to piss me off.

"Come on, somebody tell me something," I said, pacing and twirling my keys like a New York detective. An odd feeling had come over me. For once, I wasn't worried about anyone's feelings but my own. I wanted to know the truth, and I didn't care how cool I thought Aunt Emily was before, how many tears my mother shed now, or what my father did to keep the family afloat.

I wanted answers that would give me closure to a past I couldn't escape, no matter how far I moved. I wanted a life worth living—something I hadn't had in years. I didn't care how long I had to stand there. Somebody was going to tell me what all the "hush-hush" was about.

"Just tell me!" I yelled, after a few more moments of calm.

"Just tell him! Shit, he startin' to sound like you, Tony," Aunt Emily said.

"Dad, Mom, tell me something," I pleaded.

"Okay, son," my dad said, standing up. "But I think you might want to sit down."

"Just tell me," I insisted, still standing.

"Well, for starters, your Aunt Emily and I used to date, before your mother and I ever got together," he said. "We never told you, for whatever reason, but yeah, we used to date. Even after your mother and I got married, I never stopped having feelings for her. I admit to flirting a lot over the years; there was a lot of flirting back and forth, but we never acted on anything."

"So how did Mathew come to be born?" I interrupted.

"Just let me finish, son." He paused, and then continued. "One night, your mother caught us flirting and demanded a divorce, just like that," he said, snapping his fingers. "I was in shock. I mean, it was your mother, for god's sake—the woman I'd been married to for almost twenty-seven years, the woman who birthed my first son. I went everywhere looking for her, finally stopping at Emily's after my search turned up empty. Since Emily and I used to date, I considered her a good friend. You know—you've seen us together," he said, trying to convince me of his and Aunt Emily's platonic relationship.

"We started talking about why both of us had failed at our relationships. We'd had a few drinks, and while that's no excuse, one thing led to another, and—here we are." He heaved a long sigh.

"So it's just you and Aunt Emily that are to blame?" I asked. I must have misheard everything earlier. None of this was my mother's fault; all the anger I had directed towards my father was warranted.

"Nah, that's not the end of it," Aunt Emily said. "We found out, months later, that my husband, Cedric, and your 'oh, so innocent mother' had been fooling around way before anything happened between your father and me. They'd been creeping around for years." Aunt Emily turned to my mother, who began to bawl into her hands. "They had been planning to divorce us both and run off together like some damn teenagers. She looked for any reason in the world to divorce your dad. So as I see it, we're all guilty—some maybe more than others," she said glaring in the direction of my mother.

Tears began to flood my eyes. I was in the middle of a soap opera, which reminded me of why I never watched them.

"What does all this mean?" I asked no one in particular.

"That depends on you, son, but then again, it always has," my father said. "You have to decide if you can live in an untraditional family. I know you have a life in Houston, but nobody loves you down there like we do, I can promise you that. You've got a little brother who could learn a lot from his big bro." He smiled slightly. "Son, when you leave this time, just know everything is out in the open. There are no secrets. And while it's unfortunate that all this took place, we've come to grips with it and realize that we've got to deal with the now, rather than relive the past."

I wasn't sure if he'd noticed my mother's peculiar behavior over the years, but in my eyes, she hadn't come to grips with any of this. All this time, I figured she was upset because her family split up; instead, she was depressed over the untruths she'd told. She was as guilty as a politician, and the truth has a funny way of eating you up inside. No wonder she'd cried the entire time I was there.

She got up, still sobbing, and came towards me—arms open for a hug. But without so much as a flinch, I turned and walked out, angry for having to be angry in the first place, angry that she was more of a culprit than my father, but all in all—just angry.

After learning the truth, I was on the fence about keeping my promise to Leigh to see her before I left town. She would understand if I couldn't—I mean I did just find out my family was more twisted than I originally thought. What kind of company would I be, anyway? I'd been driving aimlessly for the last forty-five minutes, trying to figure it out. Maybe I should go see Victoria, I thought, as I neared closer to nowhere. Heads Leigh, tails Victoria, I wagered, taking out a quarter and flipping it in the air.

"I'll get it," I heard Leigh yell. "Who is it?" she asked, opening the door, without waiting for a response.

"Hi, Roman," she said, a surprised look on her face. "I wasn't sure I was going to see you before you left."

"I promised I was going to come by before I left, so I'm here," I snapped.

"Uh, okay," she said, sounding confused. "When are you leaving?"

"Tomorrow morning at about eleven," I said. I was being short with her, even I could tell.

"Why so soon?" she asked.

"What do you mean, so soon? I've been here almost a week now, and I got what I came for."

"And what's that?" she asked.

"I came to see if you were okay." I purposely omitted the newfound truths about my family. "Seeing my family and friends just came along with the territory. Is your arm still okay?" I asked her, noticing she seemed to be moving it a bit more freely.

"Yeah, it's fine, I tried to tell the doctors and my parents I didn't need to be baby-sat, but you know how it goes when everybody's worried about you."

I envied her. She had such a complete, structured family life.

"Oh, yeah, Roman, my parents told me to invite you to dinner before you left, to thank you for keeping an eye on me throughout the week and to give you a 'proper send off,'" she said, making quotations with her fingers.

"Who's at the door, baby?" Mrs. Anderson said.

"It's Roman, Mom," Leigh returned.

"I see that," she said, walking out into the hallway. "Hello, Mr. Roman. Did Leigh tell you about the dinner invitation we extended your way?" Before I could answer, she said, "Leigh, where are your manners? Roman, please come in," and ushered me inside.

"When are you leaving, Roman?"

When I told her, she gasped. "Tomorrow! Well, I guess we have to celebrate a little sooner than we thought. I'm going to let you guys chat while I go check on your father and Kevin," Mrs. Anderson said, exiting the room.

"I guess tonight's dinner is going to be a send off for us both 'cause there's no way I'm staying here another week, especially with you not here," Leigh said. "Plus, I've got to get back to school. I've got finals coming up, and I don't want to miss another week of class."

I heard yelling and cheering in the other room, and anger began to overwhelm me.

"Is your dad having a party or something in there?" I asked Leigh.

"No, he's just watching sports," she said.

"Him and bunch of guys, right?" I asked.

"No, it's just him and one other guy," she said, rather plainly.

"Oh, yeah, Kevin. Right. Is he like your uncle or something?"

"No, he's not my uncle," she shot back.

"Is he a close friend of your dad's?"

"No. Why are you being so nosey?" she screeched.

"Just answer the question. Who is he?" I demanded.

"He's my boyfriend, okay? He came back early from his business trip and decided to see how I was doing."

"I knew that already," I retorted. "I knew you had a boyfriend named Kevin. I was waiting for you to say something about him. You already told me about him, remember?"

"Yeah, I remember," she said. "I just didn't know if you did or not."

"He's like a traveling drug dealer or something, right?"

"Pharmaceutical sales."

"When did you plan on telling me he was here? Or did you want me to just walk in and introduce myself to him?"

"I was going to tell you he was here, I just know how—Geez, Roman, he just got here yesterday," she said.

I can't lie; I was jealous. All that time we'd spent talking, and she couldn't tell me her boyfriend was in the other room?

"Yeah, and I got here ten minutes ago. So what?"

"What's wrong with you?" Leigh asked, a sour look on her face.

"Nothing's wrong! I just—I-I don't know. I should probably just go. This wasn't a good idea."

"You think coming to see me was a mistake?" Leigh hissed. "I never asked you to come here, Roman!"

"I meant coming back to San Diego was a big mistake," I said.

"What did you expect?" she steamed.

"I expected to catch up with my friends and—I don't know—see what I had been missing while I was away."

"So you really didn't come here to see me?"

"No, I did. You're the reason I came in the first place. But there's a lot of stuff you don't know."

"You mean there's a lot of stuff you didn't tell me?" she barked.

"Well, yeah, there are a lot of things I didn't tell you about, but I didn't want to bog you or anybody else down with my problems, 'cause that's what they are—my problems."

"So what was all that you were fussing about before? How certain things about a person's life are usually included in the conversation when people are catching up after three years," she said, trying to emulate my voice. "What was it you were telling me? Were you really mad at me for not telling you I had a boyfriend, or were you being a hypocrite?"

"No, I just had some stuff I didn't want anyone to know—things that have nothing to do with your love life," I said.

"So what are they, Roman?" she said. "You can tell me. I promise, whatever you tell me stays between you and me."

I thought about her offer a moment before graciously declining. It would have been nice to have an ear, but I didn't want to open that can of worms, especially since I was leaving so soon.

"I'm sorry, Leigh, but I have to go."

"So is this your official goodbye?" she said as anger creased her forehead.

"Take care of yourself, and tell your mom I'm sorry, but I had to go. Maybe we can have dinner when I visit next time."

"So that's it? You come over for twenty ten minutes and leave things no better than they were before? You know what, Roman? I was wrong about you. You are a coward. Things get a little rough, and you run," she yelled as I walked to the front door.

I stopped in my tracks, livid. It was like she and my father had rehearsed the best ways to anger me. I also didn't like that she, of all people, was saying this to me. She was supposed to be on my side, and here she was using the C word, with me. She didn't know enough about me to say that.

I walked outside to make sure her mother, who I assumed was still in the TV room with Mr. Anderson and Kevin, wouldn't hear our conversation.

"Leigh, you don't know anything about me, not a damn thing."

"I know enough," she retorted. "I know you're leaving again, and I know there's something going on between you and your family. I do know that."

"How do you know that?" I asked, surprised at her intuition.

"I just do. I'm not stupid, Roman. I can tell when there's tension between people. I am a psychology major," she said. "But even if I wasn't, it doesn't take a rocket scientist to see that there's a problem between you and your family."

"Okay, you're right. So what? I got family problems," I announced. "Now what? Are you gonna let me borrow yours? Who wouldn't want a perfect family like yours?" I was being patronizing and, I know, infuriating.

"Whatever, Roman! Every family has problems—mine definitely does," she said. "I wanted you to tell me what's been going on because I wanted to be there for you. You've always been there for me. I wanted to return the favor."

I hated to admit it, but Leigh was right. Maybe that's where many of my problems began. I had bottled up my feelings and was living in Houston with no one to talk to, or just vent my frustrations to. And, while never the type to tell my problems to just anybody, I hadn't understood, when I left home, how much I would need a confidante, or how lonesome Houston would be.

Leigh was right. I was contradicting myself by not letting her know what was going on. Plus, I was withholding the same information from Leigh that I had briefly shared with Victoria, and I hadn't even known her a week. To not be a hypocrite, I would have to tell her everything.

So, as Leigh's parents and boyfriend sat inside the house, I opened up to Leigh like I had never done with anyone outside my mother. I told her everything and spared nothing—my living conditions (or lack there of) in Houston, the reasons I left San Diego in the first place, my anger at my father all these years, and how much it pained me that my mother played a huge roll in our family's implosion after I'd believed her an innocent victim. I even told her about Uncle Sin and the infamous episode.

She stood there, a look of sympathy and shock on her face, wondering what to say. I, on the other hand was emotionally drained. She came to me with open arms and a sad expression. As much as I hated her seeing me this way, I couldn't help but love the way it felt when I laid my head against her sturdy shoulder.

Mrs. Anderson walked out, and I jumped as though we had been doing something wrong. "How cute," she winked.

"I was wondering where you guys were. Roman, are you going to stay for dinner or not? I was going to fire up the grill in back. And I wanted you to meet Leigh's boyfriend, Kevin—that is, if I can get his and Mr. Anderson's attention away from that darn game or that kick-fighting for a minute." She smiled at Leigh.

"I guess I can stay for a while, but I have to finish packing and run a couple other errands before I leave tomorrow."

"Oh, good! I'll start the grill. Leigh you should take Roman in and introduce him to Kevin."

As Mrs. Anderson scampered away, Leigh and I were left alone to ponder our thoughts.

"Roman, I'm glad you finally told me what's been going on with you; you can always talk to me, no matter where you are. I really wish you had told me all this earlier," she said. "But I'm here. You know that right?" she asked, unsure.

"Yeah, I do," I responded.

As Leigh and I walked down the hallway, loud oohs and ahhs could be heard from the back room.

"Let me go get Kevin." Mrs. Anderson said, putting down a huge slab of thawed meat she had just taken out of the refrigerator. We waited in the kitchen. I didn't want to sit and wait for all that meat to be barbequed, but I had to see what Leigh's boyfriend looked like—it was mandatory.

Leigh stood there looking flushed as her mother retrieved Kevin from the other room.

"Roman, this is Kevin. Kevin, Roman," Mrs. Anderson said, thrusting us at each other and taking a step back, as if we were going to kick-box.

"How you doing, Roman? I've heard a lot about you," he said, extending his hand.

"Likewise." Our hands locked.

He intimidated me. He was, for lack of a better word, perfect. His face was perfectly proportioned. His haircut was flawless. With his hazel, almond-shaped eyes and cocoa skin, on a six-two or three frame, I'm sure he drove the ladies bananas. He looked like a genetically engineered version of baseball player Alex Rodriguez. He shook my hand, and smiled, showing teeth so white and uniform he could have been Lena Horn's son. I didn't have a chance; it was a first-round knock-out ten seconds into the bout.

At that moment, looking at this Adonis, I realized my feelings for Leigh. She was not "like a sister" to me, and if she was, I needed to be committed for having impure thoughts about her. I loved her—no ifs, ands, or butts about it. It was true, life altering, and immediate. No wonder we fought so much; she was the little girl on the playground picking on the boy she liked. I'd been an idiot, letting my dream woman slip away.

Mike's annoying ass was right, and I'm sure my dad must have felt the same or I wouldn't be here when he knew she wasn't in that bad a shape. The only problem was that she was in a relationship with a man that made me look like Urkel. Even though she had said she had feelings for me before, I still tried to find any flaw possible on her gorgeous boyfriend.

"I hear you're visiting from Houston," Kevin said. His face housed the wide smile that I imagined he flashed women when he flirted.

"I leave early tomorrow morning," I said as I planned my escape. "As a matter of fact, I really have to go now, or it's going to get too late to run my errands." I looked towards Mrs. Anderson. "I have to go," I repeated. Mrs. Anderson turned, her hands wet with the barbeque sauce she'd been rubbing on the meat.

"You sure you can't stay a little longer? You didn't even get a chance to taste my world famous Brazilian barbeque," she said, placing the bowl down and rushing in my direction.

"I'm sorry, Mrs. Anderson—"

'Linda,' she corrected me.

"I'm sorry, Linda, but I just have so much more to do, and so little time to do it."

"Well, that's unfortunate, but I understand," she said. "I hope you have a safe trip home, Mr. Roman, okay? Take care of your self, all right?" She wrapped her arms around me, avoiding touching me with her sauce-covered hands.

"Yes, ma'am, you do the same," I said in a muffled voice, trying to avoid her big blonde hair. "It was nice meeting you, too, man," I turned to shake Mr. Perfect's hand.

"Leigh, it's been—"

"I'll walk you out," she said, cutting me off.

"Tell Mr. Anderson I said goodbye," I screeched as Leigh and I walked outside.

"Well, I guess this is goodbye." I hugged Leigh.

"I guess it is," she said. Her eyes swelled with tears.

"I can't believe I'm leaving tomorrow. It seems like I just got here yesterday," I said.

"I know," she said with a sniffle. "Roman, I-I want you to be happy. Get the anger out of your heart. It's causing you misery. You only have two parents, and I know it's hard to imagine sometimes, but they make mistakes, too. You can either forgive them and rebuild your relationship, or stay mad and have your Uncle Sin be the only family you have. It's up to you. Talk to them and get your life back together; the only thing stopping you is you."

"I know," I said, wishing I could tell her how I felt, that I was leaving the only person I'd really talked to in years, and that I'd figured out my feelings towards her. Leigh was right, as well; I had to mend the broken relationship with my parents. This had gone on too long, and too many people had suffered because of it.

"I have to go now. Good luck, Leigh." I looked into her face. "I love you—like a sister," I added quickly, embracing her. Beads of sweat formed on my forehead. *I really have to go now*, I thought, loosening my bear hold on Leigh, although I could have held her all night. "Keep in touch." I drove away, and Leigh vanished into the night.

My heart raced the entire journey to my father's house as I anticipated our reunion. I had prepared a speech detailing everything I wanted to say on the way, but forgot as I reached the front door.

I rang the doorbell, once, then twice. *Diiing-dooong!*

When there was no answer, I pounded on the door. It wasn't even nine o'clock yet. *He can't be asleep,* I thought, ringing and pounding the door again.

I thought of calling his cell, but didn't have a need for it before tonight, so I never bothered to save or memorize his number. I called my mother, hoping to share my revelations with her, but she wasn't answering, either. When I went to her house, she wasn't home. *Where am I supposed to go now*? I thought, disappointed that my good news would have to wait.

"Hey, how have you been?" I asked Victoria when she answered the door.

"Fine," Victoria returned unenthusiastically.

"I wanted to come by and see you before I left, to say goodbye in person," I told her. I couldn't tell her my good news though, because she didn't seem excited enough for what I thought was a apocalyptic disclosure.

"Okay," she said, turning to go inside. "Have a good trip and a good life."

"Hold up, Victoria," I shouted. "What's up? Why are you acting all weird and stuff?"

"Roman, we said our goodbyes yesterday. Why are you coming over and acting like nothing ever happened?"

"I'm not trying to act like nothing happened. I'm trying to apologize before I leave," I said.

"Okay, and I'm saying thank you," she said, standing in the doorway. "So, like I said before, have a good trip and a good life."

She was really beginning to frustrate me.

"I came all the way over here to talk to you, to tell you what's been up with me and my family and 'have a good trip' is all you have to say?" I asked. "I don't understand you, Victoria. Why are you acting like this?"

"Because I've moved on, Roman," she said bluntly. "Maybe you should, too."

"Vicky, this pot is boiling over," shouted a voice from inside.

"Moved on?" I ranted. "In a damn day? How could you have moved on in one day?" I asked.

"My ex-boyfriend and I got back together last night," she said.

"Wow. All that stuff you told me about wanting to get to know me better? What happened to that?"

"You happened to all that," she shouted. "I told you how I was feeling, and you didn't even care. You just had to go home."

"Did you expect me to pack up and move here to be with you?" I asked her.

"No, but I at least wanted you to consider it," she said. "You told me how much you hated Houston—so why not come back here?"

I was done talking to Victoria. She was too irrational and snide for me. And she was beginning to deflate the good mood I'd been in.

"You know what? Now that I'm listening to you, I'm glad I never told you everything that was going on with me. Look at the way you're acting," I said.

"I guess we should have never tried to be friends in the first place," she said.

"So you don't want my friendship?"

"Friendship?" she chuckled. "We've known each other for-not even-a week. We're not friends. Friends can depend on one another, and I don't feel like I can do that with you." She looked towards the front door. "And like I said, I've moved on, so I guess this is goodbye."

I didn't care who was inside; for all I knew, it was her new boyfriend. I was more upset with Victoria and her actions towards me after all we'd talked about.

"I guess it is, Victoria; I wish you the best," I said, turning and heading for my car.

When I looked back, Victoria was standing in her doorway with a bald white man who looked like Mr. Clean.

It was unfortunate that I had to lose her as a friend, but at least it wasn't me running away this time.

13

Circus

I went home to finish packing my things, and because I had no more people to see. I flipped through channels for a while as I lay there anticipating my leaving, but also wishing I could have seen my parents and told them the good news. I thought about Leigh, Victoria, and this whole crazy ride during my stay in San Diego. With all that on my mind, before I knew it, I was asleep. Then the doorbell rang.

"Who is it?" I yelled, covering my underwear with a pair of shorts.

"It's Leigh."

I rushed to open the door.

"I was hoping it was you," I said, opening the door to Mike's grinning face.

"I was hoping it was you, too," he said, still trying to sound like a woman. "That's so sweet; you wanted to see your girlfriend, Leigh," he said, laughing.

"What do you want Mike?" I exhaled, upset that it wasn't Leigh at the door.

"Aren't you glad to see me, homie? I just came to make sure you were okay. I heard what happened between you and Victoria—tough luck, dog, 'cause damn, that girl was fine. But don't worry about it. I got a lady in the car who really wants to meet you."

"What? Come on, Mike, I ain't tryin' to meet any girls tonight. I gotta get some sleep, man. You know I'm leaving tomorrow."

"And that's exactly why you have to meet this girl tonight," he said.

"Mike, why are you doing this to me?" I pleaded.

"Just trust me," he said, walking back to his car. When the door opened and Cassandra, Michelle, JC, and to my surprise, Victoria, stepped out, as though my sidewalk were the red carpet at a major ball.

"Hi, Roman," she said. "Can we talk in private?" Instead of waiting for an answer, she walked directly to my room. "I'm so sorry for earlier. I was being such a bitch. I can't believe I acted that way. I was just really hurt. I had to come by and apologize. Even though I'm sad you're leaving, I was hoping we *could* still be friends."

"You don't need to apologize. I'm just glad you came over," I said. "I wasn't lying when I said I wanted us to remain friends."

"I know," she shot back. "I wanna be your friend, too. You're a special person, Roman; I hope you know that. You really are. I was just upset that we wouldn't get a chance to see if things could have worked between us—you know—as more than friends."

I smiled and said, "You'll be okay, Victoria. At least you've got your bald-headed ex. Shoot, back in Houston, I'd even settle for a bald-headed woman."

"Stop it," she said, waving her hand though she were shooing a fly away. "That was just Justin, and he's not my ex-boyfriend. He's Cassandra's brother. He's on leave from the Marines and came by for a visit."

"So you don't have an ex-boyfriend that you just got back together with?" I asked.

"Oh, yeah, I did lie about that, didn't I? I'm not back with anybody. I just said that to make you jealous."

Ding-dong, again, went the doorbell. I walked towards the door, but Mike was already in the process of opening it.

"Is Roman here?" I heard a voice say.

"Yeah, he's right here," Mike said with a smirk.

"Leigh? What are you doing here? I thought you left a long time ago."

"Time kinda got away from us, and Kevin likes driving at night better," she said. "Plus there were some things I wanted to talk to you about before you left. I didn't like the way we left things at my parents' house. Can we go somewhere and talk for a minute?" she asked.

"Yeah, sure," I said, walking past my room, hoping we were quiet enough not to be seen by Victoria. I walked her to the other guest room like she were contestant number two in a dating game, then quietly shut the door as Leigh began to speak.

"Roman. So. Hi," she said, followed by an uneasy smile. "I wanted to let you—well, remember all that stuff I told you before? About how much you mean to me and how much I care about you? Well, nothing's changed. I still really care about you, and there was something I wanted to tell you before you left."

"Okay, what is it?" I inquired.

"Well, I—"

Knock-knock-knock went the door. Leigh and I both turned towards it.

"Who is it?" I cautiously said, hoping the person behind the door was anyone besides Victoria.

"It's Mike," the voice said, and my heart rate calmed. "Can you come out here for a minute?"

"Hold that thought," I told Leigh as I went into the hall with Mike.

"My bad, man, I had no idea Leigh was coming here tonight. If I would have known, I wouldn't have brought Victoria here," he said.

I was trying to be angry with Mike, but I couldn't be. I knew he wouldn't have put me in a situation like this. At least, not on purpose—it was all just bad timing. *Mike and his damn surprises,* I thought as I glanced across the hall, hoping Victoria stayed put.

"I know. I just have to talk to them both and hopefully get back to Houston in one piece," I said with a queasy smile.

"I got your back. Cassandra and Michelle keep trying to come back here. They're sayin' shit like, 'I didn't know Roman was a player,' and 'Men are all the same.' But don't worry 'bout it. I got 'em in check; you just do what you gotta do!"

"I appreciate that. Last thing I need is them running back here making things more difficult than they already are. By the way, what happened the other night with JC, Cassandra, and Michelle?" I asked Mike, my curiosity sparked during the weirdest of times.

"Them hoes was just tryin' to make me mad 'cause they said I was acting a fool off that liquor."

"So you and Cassandra are cool?" I asked him.

"I hit that earlier. If we ain't cool, I can't tell," he said, grinning.

I nodded and grinned back. "Well, I guess I had better go."

"Let me know if you need me," he said, walking back to the living room.

I nodded and went back to the room where Victoria was.

I was trying my best to keep Victoria and Leigh in different rooms. "Can you hold on one second?" I would say, without an explanation, as I trotted between rooms. It was like a bad episode of *Saved by the Bell,* more so because Zack always got caught, or gave way to his conscience.

I don't know why I was so afraid of them meeting each other. Then again, women tend to be emotional, especially when they have feelings for the same man. The thought of a bikini-clad catfight crossed my mind in the hallway as I re-entered the room where Leigh was stashed.

"Where'd you go?" she asked.

I pointed behind me and mumbled, "Mike," followed by an uneasy laugh and a subtle wiping of my brow.

Trying to keep up the charade was stressful, even if it hadn't been more than ten minutes. I wasn't the smoothest satin in the basket, so it was only a matter of time before I was caught. How was I to explain Victoria and Leigh to one another? And if it were as innocent as I would have them believe, then why was I sneaking around? I wasn't sure what Victoria would do, but Leigh would have a fit, no doubt about it.

I'm just going to come right out and do it. I'm going to introduce them, I promised myself. *Yep, any second now, I was going to do it*. Moments passed slowly, it was science class all over again.

"I need something to drink," I told Victoria. She stared at me intently from the Lazy-Boy chair nestled in the corner of the room. "Do you want anything?" I asked, opening the door and waiting for a response. She shook her head no, and I walked out, making sure the door was completely closed behind me. I went down the hall and asked Leigh if she wanted a drink. She didn't. I wondered how womanizers had the energy to do it as I took a deep breath and went to get my drink and collect my thoughts.

Mike, JC, Cassandra, and Michelle were standing up and yapping away as I entered the room. Leigh's pretty-boy boyfriend was sitting in my favorite recliner with his legs crossed, drink in hand, looking pissed--like here weren't ready to go now, but *right* now.

"Rome!" Mike yelled. "What-chu gonna do?" he whispered in my ear, following me into the kitchen.

"I don't know. Come clean? I haven't done anything wrong," I said in a tone even I didn't believe.

Mike shook his head, "Goddamn, I would hate to be you. Well, maybe not *hate* to be you, 'cause both them hoes is fine—I mean women, err, young ladies," he said, correcting himself before I could.

"What am I supposed to do?"

"Man, I would call in a bomb threat, or the cops, or something. Shit, I almost hate to say it, but maybe you should tell them the truth." He sounded like he'd just realized the validity of honesty. "Either that, or get rid of one of them."

"I have to figure out something quick. I'm not suited for this sneaking around stuff. I need to get back to them." I sipped on some water and left the room.

The doorbell rang, saving me from the Victoria-and-Leigh situation.

"I bet you it's another one of Leigh's fruitcake friends," Mike chuckled as I approached the door.

I didn't want any more confrontations. My last day in town was turning into a circus, and I just wanted to chill out and rest before my early flight.

I opened the door and saw Cassandra's brother standing there. Before I could wonder what he wanted, I opened the door and told Cassandra that her brother was there.

She looked horrified and yelped, "Oh, shit!"

"What's the matter?"

"That's not my brother. That's Victoria's crazy ass ex-boyfriend," she said.

The commotion was louder than the light music, and Leigh and Victoria galloped out see what was going on--their official meeting seen but unseen.

"Oh, God. What do you want, Justin?" screamed Victoria.

Without answering, he grabbed her arm. "Let's go. We're going home."

She whipped her arm out of his grasp. "I'm not going anywhere with you. I told you it was over."

"Do we have a problem here?" Mike said, inching closer as Cassandra stepped in to keep the peace.

"No. There's no problem! Me and Victoria are going home," Justin calmly said, grabbing her arm with enough force to make her gasp. She began flailing like a kidnap victim trying to get loose.

"Let me go!" she yelled as he pulled her toward the door.

In essence, it was seven on one. Cassandra, Michelle, JC, and even Leigh were grabbing at Justin to let her go. Mike was standing back, trying to line up a good shot, but with all those people around, it was a gamble I hoped Mike wouldn't take.

While all this was happening, I shuffled towards the door. While they were tugging, pulling, and poking at Justin on Victoria's behalf, I stood in front of the door and awaited his arrival. When he finally arrived with Victoria and the rest of the gang pulling on him, like a football player trying to score a touchdown, I was blocking his entrance to the end zone.

"Move," he yelled, all of them draped over him. I didn't budge. I smelled the alcohol on his breath as he let go of Victoria. "Move," he shouted.

Once he had released Victoria, all of his would-be tacklers let him go. I had no idea what I was doing, but he had disrespected me in my own house, and I didn't take too kindly to that. I didn't have a fight in mind, but I wasn't going to just let him walk out.

"I'm gonna tell you on more time—" Before he could finish his sentence, his fist was flying towards my face. He was going to connect, and I could do nothing about it.

14

Goodbye

As loud as the commotion had been when the brouhaha ensued, it was that quiet when I came to. I was lying in a hospital bed, waiting for my blurred vision to go from triple, to double, back to single. I guess I had been awakened many times, as is the rule with concussed patients, but this was the only time I remembered actually being awake since yesterday. I blinked, staring at my gathered family and friends.

"I was looking for you guys yesterday," I said in a raspy voice to my parents, who were looking down at me. "Where were you?"

"Well," my father said, as he and my mother smiled at each other, "we were making up."

"What do you mean?" I asked.

"Your mother and I are going to be all right," he said as they again smiled at one another.

Justin had hit me with a pair of brass knuckles. Apparently, this wasn't the first time he had followed Victoria and gotten violent. He probably had it a lot worse than I did. They told me Mike whipped his ass real good before they called the police. So now he had to deal with both regular and military legal consequences.

Even though I was in a hospital bed, I felt better than I had in a long time. Seeing my mother and father standing together eased a bit of the pain from my aching head, and being able to hold my little brother and see him as just that let me know that this was a new day—and there was Leigh, standing off to the side holding a bouquet of flowers.

I set them down next to a bushel of roses and awaited her soft embrace. She hugged me as though her shoulder was completely healed—the type of hug a soldier gets upon return from active duty.

My family left the room to “find the bathroom,” but I knew it was to give Leigh and I a couple moments alone, because my room *had* a bathroom. Leigh told me she had come by my house yesterday to apologize for lying to me about her and Kevin’s relationship—apparently, her father and I were the only ones who didn’t know he was gay.

"He not ready to come out yet, so I've been his 'girlfriend' for the last year or so--it's just until he's ready," she said. She assumed I would be mad at her for lying to me. Even if it hadn’t been to make me jealous, it would have still been funny. We had to laugh at the irony. I also had to giggle at her being the second woman to lie to me about her significant other in as many days. *At least Leigh’s intentions were noble,* I thought to myself, remembering Victoria’s ex clubbing me.

Victoria was the only one who wasn’t accounted for. I’d heard from everybody else, and a part of me was offended that she hadn’t looked in on me.

“When are they letting you out of here?” Leigh asked.

“I don’t know. I’m sure they’re gonna want me to stay another night or so for observation, just to make sure no screws are loose,” I said. “Speaking of hospitals, I know exactly how you felt when you were in there. I haven’t been here a full day yet, and I already wanna go home.”

“You think it'd be okay for you to go for a little walk?” Leigh said, knowing I was supposed to be in bed. “Just for some fresh air?”

I knew it as well, but I agreed without bothering to ask the nurse. I put on some clothing and tried my best not to look like a patient.

As we walked down the hall, I saw my family heading back towards the room. After feeling like an outcast for so long, I smiled at the thought of having an actual family.

Concern and dismay were flitted across my mother's face. Before she could ask where I was going, I told her and my father that I was fine, and that Leigh and I were just going for a short walk. My father smiled and caressed my mother's arm. She turned her head and smiled at him. "Take care of my baby," she said to Leigh. Then, I stopped.

"Do you think it would be okay if I took Mathew with me?" I asked. "This would be as good a time as any for us to start getting to know each other." Without hesitation, he handed his son over, and that's when the reality of having a brother began to kick in.

"Oh, yeah. Here's the card that came with the bouquet of roses by your bed. Some girl brought it by," Mom whispered before I walked back to Leigh with my little brother in my arms. I didn't pay any attention to the card, or to whom it was from; I was just happy Mathew was taking to me so well. The three of us walked outside to a typical San Diego day—sunny and seventy-two degrees—the type of day that made the high housing prices seem understandable. I had to squint a bit as my eyes adjusted to the sun's rays.

"What's that?" Leigh asked, referring to the card in my hand.

"A get-well card, I guess," I vaguely said, handing Mathew to Leigh as I began to read.

Dear Roman,

I first want to apologize for everything that happened. I didn't want to tell you about my ex because, as you can see, he's crazy. I feel really bad for not telling you. I also wanted to tell you that I've decided to go back to school to major in marine biology. Our conversation on the beach really had a big impact on me. Lastly, I wanted you to realize all you have here in San Diego—good friends and family is some-

thing that shouldn't be taken for granted. Stop letting life pass you by before you end up like your uncle. You can have it all, Roman, but you have to be willing to stop and smell the roses.

With love,
Victoria Sandoval

PS
If I had to lose out to somebody, I'm glad it was Leigh!

I smiled to myself.

"Who's it from?" Leigh asked, seeing the smile beam across my face.

"A friend," I answered. "A really good friend."

"That's cool," she said, still holding my brother as we continued our leisurely walk. As we trotted around the greenery of the hospital garden, I thought about Victoria's card. I saw a bush full of roses—the smell dominated the air though it was sprayed from a can—and plucked from it the brightest red rose I had ever seen. It was much brighter than the rest and stood out like Michael Jackson when he preformed with his brothers. I shucked all of the thorns off its stem with a key, put it to my nose, and inhaled. I sneezed from the pollen and passed it to Leigh. She sniffed it, and then my brother grabbed it to impersonate us. He breathed it in and began sneezing.

Leigh and I laughed. He had a sensitive nose—just like his brother.

I wasn't able to stay on my feet very long. Thanks to the concussion and the added weight of my little brother, who weighed as much as a couple of bags of groceries, I was getting dizzy. I had to go back to bed.

I woke up a few times throughout the night to see different people by my bedside. It warmed me to know people actually gave a damn about me. The numbers of people who came by to check on me or called to inquire about my health were a welcome surprise. I checked out of the hospital the next day, and Leigh was still by my side. She had stayed with me the entire night at the hospital; even my parents had called it a night before visiting hours were over.

My parents picked us up shortly after and drove back to my house. I asked Leigh about her classes, and she told me not to worry; she could miss another two weeks and still get above a three-five.

I was told to get as much rest as I could and stay off my feet, which meant laying down all day and watching television. When the doctor said that in front of my mother, I knew I was in for a pampering, no matter how well I told her I felt. If football players could come back into a game after a concussion and run and hit each other, I at least felt I could stand up, walk around, and have general conversations.

"Son, I wanted to talk to you. Just me and you," she said, closing the bedroom door.

"What's up, Mom?" I asked, awaiting the inevitable drama I had become accustomed to over the years.

"I love you, boy," she said, giving me a giant hug, followed by a kiss on the forehead. "I love you so much!"

"I love you, too, mom," I said, enjoying the embrace.

"I'm so sorry for all of this; I can't begin to apologize to you for what I've done," she said, and held me tighter.

"Don't worry about it, Mom," I told her. "We can work through it. You, me, and Dad—we can be a family again. I know it's not going a traditional family, but who cares? As long as we all love and appreciate each other, it can work."

Tears began to flow from her eyes, but not like before. She seemed powerful—as if her words were coming from strength, not weakness. She seemed back to her old self—the way things were before the drama occurred.

Her weeping had begun to subside when she looked at me. "Roman, your father and I aren't getting back together."

Her words hit me hard and quick. "What? Why not?"

"Because, Roman, I'm getting married to someone else."

"Married?" I shouted. "Wh-what are you talking about?"

"I'm getting married, baby."

"To whom?" I demanded.

"Remember Uncle Eric?" she said

"Aunt Emily's ex-husband? The one you were cheating on Dad with? No, Mom, don't tell me this. Not now," I pleaded.

Tears steamed down both our faces. I was crushed.

"I'm so sorry, baby," she said, stealing another hug.

I wrestled out of her grasp. "What does this mean? Have you told Dad?"

"Yes, he's known for a long time now."

"Mom, I need some fresh air."

I went into the living room, past Leigh, who was sitting on my couch, obviously bored, looking for my father. I found him in the kitchen, sitting at the table as though he knew I would be looking for him.

"Your mother told you?"

I nodded. "What's going on, Dad? I thought you guys were working out."

"We are working out, but as friends and your parents. In that manner, we work. But as far as being a married couple, we don't," he said. "Actually, the night you came looking for us, we were having dinner. We were discussing telling you what she just told you."

"So that's it?" I said. "You guys are through, and I have no say in the matter?"

"We had to do what's best for us, and we felt this was the best thing for this family," he said.

I wanted to scream. Everything had almost been perfect—or perfect as it could be—and then this had to happen. I stormed out of the kitchen like an angry adolescent. I passed my mother and Leigh, who had to have heard everything, and fled out the front door, my mother and father's calls driving me to greater speed. *Who do these people think they are?* I thought.

I began walking. I had no idea where my stroll was taking me, but anything was better than being in that house. I flashed back to the day they told me they were splitting up. My father's voice echoed through my head like an empty cave: "*Son, I have bad news…*" I kept walking, passing newly painted houses, sprinklers soiling green lawns, and an actual white picket fence. I passed Mo's house and knew he and Earl were smoking weed because the garage door was only partially open. *Half past mast in their world*, I thought. I hadn't been walking a full minute when I heard Leigh behind me.

"Hold on, Roman. Dang, you walk fast."

I stopped, already knowing what she was going to say, letting her have a crack at soothing me.

"You know, you supposed to be in bed, resting," she said with a wry smile, trying to lighten the mood.

"Leigh, just go back and have my parents take you home," I told her.

"No, Roman. I'm not leaving you like this, not after everything we've been through and talked about."

"You might as well just go. There's no helping me or this family."

"What's that supposed to mean?" she asked.

"Nothing. Just—nothing."

"Roman, you need to come back and talk to your parents. You can't just bail when things get rough. Life doesn't work like that. I understand that you're angry with your parents, but if this is how you're gonna solve every problem that comes your way—"

"Then what?" I asked, knowing what she was going to say.

"Then you're gonna be on the run for the rest of your life."

I sat on the Osterman's brick wall—a family I knew still lived there because of the early seventies Cadillac which had inhabited the driveway for as long as I could remember. I thought about what she said for so long that she asked if I was all right.

"I'm going back to your house. I hope you make the right decision," she said. I stared at nothing and ignored her as though I were meditating.

She and Victoria had given me the same sound advice. While it was good advice, I just wasn't sure about things anymore. Hours ago, I was willing to accept a non-traditional family. But, how did they expect me to react when they kept dumping more garbage onto my life? Landfills have their limits too. I couldn't believe I was thinking it, but I wanted to go home, back to Houston, which is exactly what I told my parents when I walked in a half-hour or so later.

"What do you mean you wanna go home?" Leigh blurted.

"Yeah, what's going on, son?" my father asked.

I was as calm as a hostage-negotiator when I said, "I'm not strong enough to keep going through this. The next thing you guys are gonna tell me is that one of you is having a sex change, or that you aren't really my parents. I don't wanna constantly have to deal with all this madness--It shouldn't have to be like this."

"So…" my father said, his palms turned upward, like paintings of Jesus I've seen plastered across the walls of many of my older relatives' homes.

"I'm going back to Houston to live my life the way I want to live it," I said.

I saw the disappointment on their faces—especially Leigh's. I didn't really want to leave, but this was how it had to be. At least I wasn't angry anymore. I was actually happy knowing the truth, even though it meant having to leave things behind. At least this time, I had the opportunity to make an adult decision based on truths, not deceit.

I went into my room to finish packing. Moments later, Leigh stormed in.

"What the hell, Roman? Why are you being like this?" she said angrily.

"I'm just doing what I think is best for me," I told her.

"And what is that? Strip clubs with your uncle? What do you plan on doing out there, anyway?"

"That's what I'm going to find out. When I first moved, I was so angry that I wasn't willing to put myself out there. This time, I plan on doing a lot more," I said.

"Whatever, Roman," she said, storming out.

I loved Leigh and wanted to go after her, but I couldn't—not this time. I couldn't allow myself to be sucked in by her deep brown eyes. My decision was firm, and I wanted to keep it that way.

I stayed in my room a long while and was surprised that nobody else came in to change my mind. When I walked into the living room later, my parents were still there, but Leigh was nowhere to be found.

"Her parents came and got her twenty-minutes ago," my mother said before I could ask. She told us to tell you goodbye."

"I found another flight for tomorrow morning at 8:45. Can one of you guys take me?" I asked. They shook their heads in unison, as if they were boycotting speech with me.

I went back to my room and shuffled through my things, telling myself I was making the right decision. I tried to call Leigh three times, but she didn't answer.

My parents left without saying goodbye, and I was left to contemplate my life decisions alone that night.

I awoke the next morning early. I didn't have an alarm clock, but figured it around 6:30 without the help of my cell-phone clock. I tried to get out of the sun's path for close to fifteen minutes then gave up. *My last morning in SD,* I thought to myself, looking around my room and out the window--the golden sun pouring over another beautiful day. I watched a bit of early morning news, then scrounged together a "healthy" breakfast of eggs and tortilla chips. I showered, dressed and then made sure my belongings were in order, checking the closet and under the bed once more, though it were a hotel room. I was hauling my luggage to the living room when the doorbell rang.

I was shocked to see Leigh standing at my front door. "Let's go," she snapped. I walked to my car and saw my father driving it. I opened the trunk and had to put my luggage on top of duffle bag, which looked a lot like the one Leigh had brought down from LA.

On the drive to the airport, the car was silent. It seemed more like a funeral ride. As we pulled up to the courtesy drop-off area, I got out of the car, still waiting for a word from either my dad or Leigh. It was like riding in the car with secret agents.

"So, um, I guess I'll see you guys later," I said, grabbing my bags out of the back.

"Wait," Leigh said, following my footsteps and grabbing her duffle bag out of the trunk. I thought she was going to throw it in the back seat, but to my surprise, she smiled. "Ready to go?"

"What?" I asked, confused.

"Are you ready to go?" she said, grabbing her bag and stepping onto the sidewalk.

"Are you flying back to LA?"

"No, I'm going to Houston," she said matter-of-factly as she leaned into my father's window to hug him goodbye.

"Have a good flight, and a good time in Houston," my father said, as though Leigh's trip was common knowledge.

Before I could ask him what was going on, he had rolled up his window and pulled off without so much as a wave or handshake.

I was dumfounded. Leigh was going to Houston. For a second, I seriously thought I might have been dreaming, but realized that in a dream, she would have been naked, or I would have super powers and have been able to fly myself home. I didn't need to be pinched to realize that this was no dream.

"Let me see your itinerary," I demanded, almost snatching it out of her hand. I checked it; she was indeed going to Houston and on the same flight as I.

If this was a trick, it was an expensive one.

“Too bad we’re not sitting next to each other,” she said when I handed it back to her.

“Come on, Leigh. What’s going on?”

“Well, if you’re going to run again, I’m going to follow you, and you can be partially responsible for my failing the quarter. But it’s okay; we’ll have a good time in Houston. I heard there’s a lot of opportunity out there.”

I had to smile at her attempted guilt trip, and the fact that she was a terrible actress.

I was going to press the issue a little bit, but I wanted to give my mother a call before I left—just to be a good son. I took out my phone to call her and noticed I had a new message. I checked it and heard a familiar voice yelling at the top of his lungs.

“Nephew, where the hell you been? Houston ain’t been the same without you. Yeah, but anyway, I got good news for you, nephew. Ya favorite uncle’s getting hitched. Yep, I said it. Hitched. I’m retirin’ my jersey and turnin’ in my playa card, He-he-he. Uh-huh, and she fine, too. Matter of fact, we just got to Vegas a couple hours ago. We may do the deed here or not, but either way, it's gonna go down. Gimme a holla when you can, we ‘bout to go, he-he-he--well, you know how I do it. Wish you was here! Yeeeaahhh girl—wrap them long legs ‘round daddy!

Now, I really gotta go. Later, nephew!”

I looked at my phone, the screensaver of my little brother staring me in the face like an unmistakable omen, and then at Leigh. At Leigh and then my phone. My uncle's voice echoing in my head like a hangover.

Houston ain’t been the same without you!

I didn't get on the plane that morning. And neither did Leigh.

Printed in the United States
92910LV00002B/151/A